KRISHNA CIRCUS

MADHUREETA ANAND is a multifaceted author, entrepreneur, film-maker and activist. Her films have garnered both national and international recognition, winning prestigious awards such as the Silver Conch at the Mumbai International Film Festival and the Best Foreign Film award at the Xian Film Festival in China. In addition to her cinematic achievements, Madhureeta contributes to various websites and magazines, and her writings are featured in the anthologies 'Search for Sita' and 'Finding Radha'. As an advocate for women's and children's rights, she founded Phree For Safety, a globally available mobile application dedicated to women's safety.

KRISHNA CIRCUS

MADHUREETA ANAND

Om Books International

First published in 2024 by

Om Books International

Corporate and Editorial Office
A-12, Sector 64, Noida 201 301
Uttar Pradesh, India
Phone: +91 120 477 4100
Email: editorial@ombooks.com
Website: www.ombooksinternational.com

Sales Office
107, Ansari Road, Darya Ganj
New Delhi 110 002, India
Phone: +91 11 4000 9000
Email: sales@ombooks.com
Website: www.ombooks.com

ISBN: 978-93-6395-480-9

Printed in India

10 9 8 7 6 5 4 3 2 1

For my father Lt Col. V.K. Pachauri,
sister Madhavi Anand Shergill and sweet mama Sarita Anand

In death we are all superheroes.
Lighting up the afterlife.

Contents

Preface

All superhero tales have backstories. In the coming pages, you will read a few of these but it is the backstory of *Krishna Circus* the book which is as extensive if not as fantastical.

I moved to Mumbai to make my first feature film. All of it was miraculous, a recently single mom and film-maker makes her first feature film. I wrote the script sitting in bed in New Delhi, late at night, next to my sleeping daughter. And now the film was in production – in a turn of fate, my imagination would now have the lease of public life. Naturally then, I threw myself at it and gave it my all. It was unexpected and new, including the film's story which involved an imaginary lover who becomes the leading lady's conduit to finding her voice and becoming a singer. The imaginary lover's arrival on screen transformed her home from prosaic to poetic. It was 2008 and special effects were complex and out of our budget. So, we brought in poster painters who formerly painted film hoardings. Earlier, these artists were much in demand when each Friday a new hand-painted visage would announce the latest Bollywood film. Over time, these hoardings, bursting with colour and drama, were replaced by printed versions.

These long-forgotten artists were more than happy to bring to life the world of the dream lover. The paintings were large, luxurious and strangely lifelike. *Krishna Circus* was born as I stood in front of one of these paintings. This one was a particularly realistic landscape of a row of trees in a lush green field. Drawn by its simplicity, it felt like a portal to a time when rows of trees and lush gardens were commonplace. It gave rise to a story about a time-travelling superhero who would save nature and Earth from destruction. For about four months, this story ran through my head till I just had to write it, but at this time Krishna was a man and it was a film script. I had been in Mumbai long enough to know that films with male leads were easier to fund but not long enough to know that *Krishna Circus* was ahead of its time. The story usually received glass-eyed nods and no further interest. I wrote half and, discouraged by the response, set it aside.

Five years later and I just could not let go of the story. One day, while I was sitting in a Gurgaon cafe attempting to write the script again, a fellow writer who lives in New York surprisingly walked in. She said out loud what I subconsciously knew to be true: 'I think you really want to write a female superhero.' I accepted that she was right and then there was no looking back.

The Pandemic came along and the script became the book you're about to read. In effect, this story has been in the works for sixteen years!

And it couldn't be a better time for it. The 'One Great Myth' idea has found new meaning in a world hurtling towards uniformity. Mythologies are no longer as freewheeling; heroes and their thousand faces increasingly contain within them a diktat. This new framework is much like the 'Lakshman Rekha', the line drawn on the ground by Ram's brother Lakshman in order to block anything that might muddy Sita's purity. There is now an imaginary line that separates the mainstream myth and what are considered 'fringe' stories. The majority view has become the authority that disapproves and controls anything outside the hard lines. But mythologies should accommodate a variety of truths and acknowledge changing times. Questions of gender, ecology and contemporary existential conflict need a franker integration into our legends.

Krishna Circus steps over the line and tells it not necessarily as it was told but as it was heard.

Writing can be a lonely pursuit. Fortunately, there are many who have encouraged and supported the process. My soul sister Sameena Zehra bravely attempted to be the book's first editor. Gratitude to my cousin Shonali Pachauri for always believing in me and being the first to encourage me to write a novel. And thanks to my sister Mandakini Pachauri for her diligent and authentic opinions. Selina Sheth, thank you for reading many iterations of the book and providing incisive yet compassionate feedback. My daughter Eka heard the story hundreds of times and never tired of it. Her continued wonderment reiterated that the story was worth telling. My mother Sarita proudly held up the first manuscript of the book and asked to be photographed. The onset of Alzheimer's meant that she could no longer read something lengthy, but she kept it under her pillow (perhaps imagining that osmosis could replace reading) and guarded it zealously. She insisted she loved every word in the book.

Publishers can either make it easier for authors or not – thank you Ajay Mago for doing the former. Also thanks to Shantanu Ray Chaudhuri. Special gratitude for Prema Govindan for being an editor extraordinaire. Deep appreciation for the Om International team: Soumya and Mohd Arif.

And finally, gratitude for my perseverance which has served me well. Wherever that came from, I hope it stays.

Prologue

Mohini

AD 2124
MATHURA, INDIA

The bird's-eye view has a different connotation when it's not a metaphor. It brings compulsory clarity. Not imagined, not presumed, not deduced, but absolute and all-encompassing. The mechanised eyes, body, wings and software for brains saw to it. Clarity is what it's all about but objectivity was as defined by the monarch himself.

This placed great responsibility on Garud's faux-feathered shoulders. He mulled this over as he cruised above luscious, undulating wilderness adorned with rivers, blooming flowers and gracefully arched branches yielding fruit that offered itself for picking. He marvelled at the perfection of the human-made wonderland. Much like himself, all of it was an exquisite replica of nature's now-extinct creations, but without its imperfections. With no pressure to evolve – bulging tree trunks, squelchy mud, oozing animal sores, and smells of bodily fluids had all been done away with.

Garud glanced at his golden-brown wings, fluttering in the light reflected off the dome's edge. It made him glisten – designed to match the gleaming domes, minarets and arches of gold of the monarch's palace – and he felt reassured. He hovered lazily, letting his mechanised eyes relay that all was well in the land of Mathura. With a shrill call, he drew attention to the creatures in the sky and forced those on the ground to look up and confront the absence of the infinite. Still, they had to look because he was their eye in the sky. Flamboyantly flapping his ample wings, he made the gold-embroidered flags flutter atop the palace and surged onwards, propelled by the very, very important mission – to survey the city and report. All the time, the algorithms hummed and learnt to make the relay more efficient. Of late, he was realising the weight of ever new knowledge and he fleetingly wondered when his dispassion had started to wane. Were machines capable of the emotional stirrings of bio-bodies? The thought made him shudder and flap in dread.

A turn later, his unconstrained aerial view revealed the simmering embers. The remains of the fire that shook years of machine learning and the people of Mathura. Scanning through stored memory, he recognised the fire as the work of forces fighting for mortality and death. It was a ridiculous and illogical war fought on behalf of Mother Nature.

Before these saviours arrived, Mother Nature fought tooth and nail. Her weapons were fire, flood, pestilence, drought and all other calamities. But it wasn't a war among equals. After all, what can beat immortality? What can beat perfection? What can beat the fulfilment of every single conceivable desire?

The sight of a perfect city that had been engulfed in flames and its surviving embers sparked something new in Garud's programmed soul – the recognition that desire was imperfection and it had Mathura in its vice-like grip. Garud knew from his gigabytes of experience that in the years gone by, creatures in the sky were buoyed by the breeze. They used to sail like ships in the sea, riding waves and going where it took them. And he missed what he had never known. He craved the wind and its endless unpredictability.

Shuddering away the longing, Garud flew low to take a good look at a shining structure. The old, abandoned baby-food factory was usually concealed using a hologram of the forest. Today it stood exposed in all its glory. From his vantage point, Garud saw thousands of citizens working in tandem with the background score of humming machines and light motivational music.

Garud's last relay announced this harmony. His job was done for the day.

Inside the building, without the benefit of a bird's-eye view, the inhabitants saw things differently. The factory which was approximately the size of two football fields was lined with a labyrinth of white metal vestibules. Each part inaccessible to the other, the curious structure was designed to obscure. On the east side, thousands of cauldrons overflowing with metallic fluid bubbled, sending up plumes of grey smoke. The west was stacked with an uncountable number of sheets of high-quality glass so clear that one had to know it was there to see it. The south and north were walled off with opaque metal barriers, keeping even sound out.

It was the lighting that brought creative flair – fluorescent colours beamed down in geometric shapes, making it look less like a factory and more like a nightclub.

The real intention of the space was confirmed by the faceless, toiling people in it. The workers labouring like ants but without the dignity or sense of purpose of the creatures were oppressed by the extreme heat and their current circumstances. Still, they only stole looks with backs bent and eyes askance; hoping to invoke a unified response while knowing full well that there was not going to be one. They had made the trade-off and were now beholden to it. They placed sheets of glass on the machine and tried to hold on to the barely visible, smudged images of themselves as they swam away on a humming conveyor belt. They wondered, in unison, when it was that an obviously good choice became a glaringly bad one.

There was only one, *the* person, who looked neither askance nor weary nor tentative nor defeated. She looked as if the coin toss would always fall in her favour and she was destined to always land on her feet. On official documents, Mohini's gender description was transgender. Still, she preferred the Indian nomenclature 'Ardhanarishwar' – the one who was wholly male and female in perfect and equal measure – a flawless balance. Her commitment to both sexes made her who she was – completely integrated with no halves involved here – Mohini was yin–yang and Shakti–Shiva equally.

Mohini, with the long limbs, aquiline nose, lustrous hair and almond-shaped eyes, was disturbingly beautiful in an otherworldly way, and entirely at ease in this one. She had recently and very mysteriously emerged from the usually non-existent shadows of Mathura. Here, where even breaths were accounted for, Mohini had somehow managed to go unnoticed so far – you see, she was awaiting her time, marking the spot for the right moment. She admired power from afar like a fan would a star. She observed it. Obsessed over it. Then, when she had the chance, she swiftly stepped up and into a position of power. Now she was rocking this new-found authority as if it had been hers all along.

Mohini rearranged the nine yards of golden fabric she was draped in and urged the workers in a gentle but commanding tone. The one hundred glass bangles on her wrists tinkled as she waved her hands to speed them up: 'Come on … keep moving. We have no time to lose.'

Mohini pitied these minions but believed they had forfeited their chance at mercy long ago. She felt neither remorse nor guilt at driving them hard, and she was willing to go within an inch of their never-ending lives to get it done. Only she truly understood what was at stake.

The workers felt their eyes smarting and thought it might be an emotional response to the extreme situation. *Perhaps we are not immune to feelings,* they thought collectively; but, after a brief and brisk mental consideration, reconciled to the fact that there were no feelings involved. It was the infernal liquid that was making their eyes water. They surreptitiously tried to touch it through hands sheathed in gloves; they peered hard and twitched their nostrils to identify it; but none could tell what it was. The grey slipping and sliding river of chemicals sashayed its way down the assembly line, dripped and spread itself generously on a waiting surface. While one set of workers, their brows creased, moved the sheets of glass, another group, their mouths set in a grimace, positioned them under the cauldrons before the turnstile moved them behind an opaque steel curtain. After a tour through the hidden north and south sections, they emerged as unimaginably large pieces of something wrapped and concealed. The pile grew with every portion that emerged. As did Mohini's smile.

Forty-eight hours later, there was no end in sight. The exhaustion and simmering resentment were wearing the workers down. The group decided they distrusted Mohini because while they dripped sweat and struggled with sleep and backaches, she looked like she had just stepped out of an oyster. Every now and then, she would quiver and dust herself lightly as if she were unravelling from the cotton wool she had previously been wrapped in. The workers – their skins dripping with perspiration, hair stuck to their scalps, and their even breaths getting raspier by the minute – resented Mohini most for these terrible imperfections that she had thrust upon them while she remained ensconced in perfection.

You see, the residents of Mathura had come to expect the monotony of perfection, but the last few weeks had considerably dented that prospect of nothing ever changing. They felt cheated and exposed. Yet they continued because there was no option. They responded to orders as they had always done. They were not questioning, not protesting – daring to complain only through downcast eyes.

Unmindful of their dissatisfaction, Mohini drove them on while breaking not a single drop of sweat. Frankly, she didn't give a damn!

Chapter 1

The Last Exodus

AD 2099
MATHURA, INDIA

Creation has shrugged her shoulders, flipped its middle finger and decided to leave humans to stew in their self-created misery. Stupid creatures that thought they had trapped the wild in ropes of greed. From time to time, she had resorted to the knuckle rap – disease, floods, storms, earthquakes and even swarms of pests. But did they learn? Did they learn? Instead, they waged a full-scale war on her. Her! Her?

It was not the first time that these thoughts flooded Devaki's mind. They had become a circular, repetitive rant that never went away – playing in the background like a bad song stuck in her head, they just went away and returned like a revolving conveyor belt. She rarely managed to coax them into a temporary state of rest. But today, the exhaustion had unshackled them entirely, and they raged unchecked as she looked at the ravaged remnants of what used to be a flowering wonderland. Now, underneath the film of dust that sheathed its surface, it flushed hot like a caged dragon breathing fire, smarting at the abuse inflicted upon her.

Devaki searched the horizon covered with columns of smog and wondered where she would get her next breath from. And breathe she must, she thought as she looked down at her swollen belly just moments away from fruition. This would be the seventh foetus that would make its way out of her body. The others before this were murdered by pollution, disease and war. She was determined to save this one. *This one* must *live*, she thought. Devaki ignored the rancid smell of decay that filled her nostrils and stroked her belly. Reassuringly, she felt something she had not felt before. Something so special that it gave her the very thing that everyone around her was fast losing – hope. She expanded her lungs, sucked in the meagre supply of oxygen, and continued to make her way up the steep mountain.

On the other side of this incline was a mythical land that none had seen. Only stray whispers carried news of the mighty, great Kams and his kingdom Mathura, where they said clean air could be breathed in gulps, water flowed unchecked, ripe fruit adorned trees, cows' udders overflowed with sweet milk, and people left food uneaten. It was the land of the immortals where there was no strife, no war – just an unending sea of peace.

Spurred by this vision, Devaki energetically put one foot after the other, and a searing cramp gripped her calves. She did want to rub them but couldn't summon any more energy. She felt herself swaying as she grabbed Vasu's arm.

Vasu – the love of her life and father to all her children. Those no longer living and the one who could. She looked at his tall, lean, long-limbed frame and thought about when they lived in harmony, surrounded by nature. Vasu's arms, now stripped of any muscle, were still rippling with the determination that made him lead them to the land of plenty and the only place on Earth where they could survive. His skin was dry, his hair greying and brittle, but his gentle soul shone through those slightly droopy eyes. Devaki thought about how much she loved him.

Vasu felt Devaki's hand on his arm and turned to support her in a response ingrained in his muscle memory. He looked at this doe-eyed, sharp-featured, diminutive woman with skin one could euphemistically describe as translucent. Sometimes he thought he could see the blood flowing in her veins. Today, every tendon in her body was visible as she clenched his arm in a bid to keep going. Vasu should have been worried about her, but this seemingly delicate woman hid within her an indomitable will. He looked at her as she hauled herself up the hill – dishevelled, her lips parched, gasping for every breath as if the world's fate depended on it; and Vasu caught what she was oozing – faith.

His heart brimmed with love, which dimmed to dismay as his gaze shifted to the horde of his fellow citizens who trailed Devaki – hundreds of thousands of tired, broken people, dragging their bodies towards a sliver of salvation.

The preceding twenty years had been the last straw on the back of Planet Earth. With the warp and weft of her disappointment and rage, she weaved a large shroud of bereavement and retreated within its fold, taking with her the possibility of rejuvenation and birth, leaving behind only devastation and death. She was awaiting a time when better creatures would roam her domain.

It all started when the Jamakhors won the battle for resources. There were Jamakhors in every part of the world. United by their strong need to hoard and devour any and every earthly resource available. Consequently, they made alliances across borders of religion, race and even gender. They pillaged the hard-working while pointing fingers at the Baharias or the outsiders. The gladiatorial pursuit of the Baharias became a riveting story of battles fought on behalf of wretched, faceless people who toiled for a pittance while distracted by this theatre of war. The Baharias pleaded for respite, but the target was not taken off their backs. In fact, their begging only egged the Jamakhors on. So they turned up the octave – and with it, the entertainment quotient. Rocked into this sweet slumber of hate, the world went on spinning. The somnolence broke when the Jamakhors fell upon each other. You see, they hoarded and hoarded, but could get no satisfaction. Plus, each of the Jamakhors thought themselves as invincible as their propaganda made them out to be.

They began eyeing each other's bounty. Space seemed to shrink before everyone's eyes as they all wanted more. Every person, every tree, every rock, every title just had to be had. It became clear that the one with the maximum will to grab power would win.

It wasn't surprising at all that Kams had won that round. His brilliant mind had started planning the end of the world way earlier than it happened. Before things began plummeting faster than fast, he had built his city, encased in an impenetrable dome. He created an idyllic world where he gave his subjects what no one else could – immortality. He chose an elite group and hid inside the dome with 'his' people, in a world where their limbs would be supple, their skins glowing, and the fountain of youth would be forever gushing. Frozen in the climax of their lives, the people of Mathura now lived in a perpetual state of full bloom. They lived (happily or not) ever after in the thrall of youth.

Outside the dome, a woman whose dry occasional hacking cough had punctuated their thirty-day journey was now gasping. There was no oxygen left for her to breathe, and she collapsed, hitting the dry and dusty ground with a thud that echoed through the treeless expanse. Her fall scattered the gravel near her open mouth, still expecting some breathable air. She inhaled a long, raspy breath and gulped a gust of mud instead. Her windpipe clogged and her nostrils were unable to fight this battle for a single breath. She flailed, convulsed, gasped and finally gave up. Her husband – dehydrated, hungry and depleted – did the only thing he could: he stared at his beloved and cried. His mouth opened, emitting loud sobs, eyes straining in grief, but he couldn't summon a single tear for the woman he loved.

Devaki first stood still, transfixed by the tragedy, and then sank to the ground, defeated. She closed her eyes to talk to an entity who was not in evidence of late. '*Listen … weren't you supposed to save us? You promised to protect us in exchange for prayer. And pray we did! Didn't we? Come on, don't prove yourself a liar. These people are depending on you, goddamit!'* She looked up, where it was believed the entity resided – and faced an opaque haze.

Vasu looked at his wife sunk in the mud, her eyes raised and her lips moving imperceptibly, and he thought: *Dear Devaki, if you give up, we all give up too.* He bent forward and patted her stomach with loving strokes, as if rubbing a lamp to conjure up Devaki's genie of hope. It seemed to work as she lowered her gaze to her belly and placed her hand on Vasu's.

Perhaps spurred by the double touch, a tiny fist rose that pushed at the nearly transparent lining of Devaki's stomach, and for a moment, there was a family high-five across placental fluid. Consequently, Devaki smiled and lit up Vasu's whole world.

Devaki drew on her reserves and forced a few steps. Vasu summoned his strength and hauled her forward in one swift movement, and there they were – at the top of the mountain. Bent from the effort, the duo straightened themselves and looked into the distance. What they saw was like the first showers of monsoon on parched earth. There it was, the glittering dome of promise. Vasu turned to share the sight with the crowd kept alive only by his word. 'I see it! Yes, it's here. There are tall trees, flowering plants, and people walking and breathing freely. It's much, much larger than I imagined. It shines, gleams, and all inside is alive. Ah, Mathura at last!'

Those that tailed Vasu rippled with anticipation, and a loud cheer went through the crowd that sounded like a thunderclap emanating from the earth.

Chapter 2

Kams

'Where are their fine lines and grey hair?' 'How is a man supposed to get excited looking at this porcelain perfection?' 'Why was it exciting before, and why is it so boring now?'

These questions swirled in the mind of Kams, the monarch of Mathura. He would have slapped himself if he had had these thoughts at another time when immortality was but a dream.

A large swarthy man, his dark hair cascading below his shoulders, muscles rippling under his well-oiled gleaming skin, his eyes drooping, mouth hung open in expectation, he lay semi-dressed in a bed large enough for an orgy. The red satin sheets were so perfect that they refused to crumple even as six women of the same size but different hues put their entire weight behind trying to turn him on. They wriggled, they squealed, they moaned, they giggled, they stroked, they rubbed, they were grinding, pressing, kissing, slapping, pinching, shouting and whispering. In addition, they tried drinking, snorting, smoking, inhaling ... and yet, like the satin sheets, nothing changed.

Exhausted but emboldened by substances, one of them asked in a whisper: 'Should we bring in the boys?'

The words sluggishly turned into images in Kams's hazy mind – flashes of the tautness that would grip him, the firm torsos, muscular legs and the possibility of dominating the strongest of them all, and the effect was? Well, nothing!

The truth is that when Kams had visualised this new, perfect world where he ruled everything, including death, he hadn't factored in the ennui.

He wanted to be at the top of the heap of the Jamakhors. It was a pitched battle. The fight for resources was at its peak and everyone had the same will to kill, along with a ruthless disregard for the have-nots. It even looked like Kams might lose, but he held on to a thin thread dangled from the realm of the stars. His army had not just warriors, metallurgists, strategists, scientists, spin doctors and real doctors, but astrologers too.

That said, his army of seers was dwindling, for he regularly executed the ones unable to predict accurately. The result was that he had a small but quality set of stargazers with legendary expertise and instinct spurred by the will to stay alive. These fortune-tellers had predicted that Kams would indeed rule the world. It was less an augury and more a cosmic certainty as far as they were concerned. Kams took this seed of hope and created a large harvest that became the glorious city of Mathura enclosed in a special protective dome.

Kams had convinced himself that it was his acumen that had positioned him as the king of the world. In reality, it was a twist of fate that changed everything. The debauchery and tedium may have blurred many memories, but that day was still clear as crystal in his mind.

Kams was always irked by Parshuram's saccharine-sweet ideals. He would have put a bullet through his head a long time ago except for the fact that Parshuram regularly brought him baubles that helped emphasise his kingdom's superiority. Parshuram was a genius – notches above the prevailing intellectual curve – because he could meld imagination with some solid science. For example, he created objects that looked just like trees, down to the last detail, such that they produced oxygen and grew as living beings could. Then he built a fortification for Mathura in the form of a see-through dome that one could enter only with a unique identification code. The list of Parshuram's marvellous creations was long, but nothing surpassed that which he brought on the day that changed everything!

When Parshuram walked into Kams's court 'that day', Kams had his head bent down and cocked – a listening stance that feigned that he was paying attention, and also served to hide his irritation. It did not help that Parshuram presented himself wearing his usual costume of ordinary hand-spun clothes at his gilded court. Parshuram's idealistic, erect neck was an anomaly amongst a sea of lowered ones, and his unhesitant speech displayed his annoying lack of fear. Kams clenched his fist in preparation for what he expected to hear. Then Parshuram told Kams what he had discovered. His hanging head was propelled up at a crick-inducing speed when he realised that Parshuram had found the key to immortality. Almost immediately, Kams began to savour the vision of vanquished enemies and prostrate humans living to his will, but then Parshuram went on to describe how he would use the path-breaking technology to regenerate nature. That all of Earth could once again have the resources it had lost, and added that he did not want this discovery to be 'misused'.

Kams was always amazed at the liberal intellectuals. *Was this naivety, or was it just plain stupidity born out of the lofty idea that everyone wanted 'peace' when, in actuality, all everyone really wanted was 'pieces' of the pies of power and wealth.* The thought spurred laughter that almost made its way to his mouth; but Kams caught it in his throat, cleared it with authority and spoke in a deep voice, booming with seeming sincerity.

'I congratulate your genius,' he said.

On cue, his sycophants applauded, simultaneously and boisterously, not paying heed to the fact that they were interrupting their master as he carefully crafted a web for Parshuram. Kams raised his hand and stopped them. In the silence that followed, he said, 'We are fortunate to have a mind like yours. Please rest assured that you are our respected elder, and we would never betray you and your most admirable ideals.'

He then stood up and, with great flair, started clapping for Parshuram. The entire court followed suit and gave him a booming ovation.

No prizes for guessing that Kams took the formula from Parshuram and used it in every way possible – fair and foul.

Kams set about collecting a race of people – those he deemed could live in his dome where there was plenitude and eternal youth. He grew more and more powerful and indeed came to rule the world. Turns out, the soothsayers were right, and he ought to have celebrated it; but then there was the other augury.

In his select assembly of astrologers was Rudra, who had a particular trait that made him both loathsome and fearsome – he never lied. This, combined with the fact that he was an excellent astrologer, made him Kams's least favourite. While all the astrologers agreed that Kams would rule the world, Rudra added a caveat. He said (and it must be quoted verbatim): 'Kams, if you choose to rule the world by using unethical means, be warned that in your kingdom will be born an avatar, a saviour, with extraordinary powers. The Messiah that will finish you and restore order to the world will be called Krishna.'

Kams spoke deliberately and softly: 'I am already restoring order in the world – can't you see?'

Rudra stood up, turned his back to Kams and spoke: 'No, Kams, you are consumed by a desire to be all-powerful, and yet no one can be more powerful than the universe. It is certain that Krishna, the alluring dark one, will come, and you will be destroyed.'

No longer able to keep the veneer of calm, Kams pulled out his gun to shoot Rudra. Still, only heaven knows what otherworldly power was at work, for Rudra disappeared, never to be seen or heard of again, leaving behind an augury that hung in the air of Mathura forever.

Kams did not want to give any credence to Rudra's ill-spoken stupid words, but he thought it wise to be safe than sorry. So, he decreed, 'Those living in Mathura must not have the capability to reproduce. Having progeny is against the law here, and anyone found to still be capable of reproducing will be served a death sentence.'

Consequently, there were no children in Mathura. Because a populace driven by the love of immortality would not do anything to bring death to their doors. So here they were – only eternally youthful adults with the possibility of having every other desire satiated, except reproduction.

In the years after, Kams established Mathura in the dome, using his entire might towards securing his beloved city. He trusted no one, especially the Baharias, who came looking for refuge from fast collapsing Earth. Kams took great pleasure in exterminating them. To start with, he concocted a reason. Sometimes it was religion, at other times, it was race or even the region they came from. But later, his mere irritation was enough. Being all-powerful meant he could throw away the pretend moral compass altogether and finally admit to himself that the bloodshed highly entertained him. Each time a crowd hit the dust, it served as a trophy to his power.

As the years went by, the crowds thinned, and there were fewer and fewer people looking for refuge. Strangely, Kams missed them and wondered if he had overpowered everyone and everything. *Am I God?* This thought brought profound tedium.

While he was battling impotence born of this very boredom, his ministers waited for him to emerge out of his melancholy so that they could once again play the farce of consensus. They looked at each other but had nothing to say. As a result of Kams's complete control and erasure of history, they had long since forgotten Rudra's augury and lost hope that anything would change. Ever.

Parshuram sat at the very end of the row of puppet courtiers. Only his white beard and greying hair betrayed that he stopped aging at about sixty years of age. His body was still strong, and his skin glowed from the machinations of his formula for youth and immortality. While he may have stopped his body from ageing, his back was bent with remorse and deep-seated hate for Kams and his trickery. He carried the heavy weight of betrayal on his back. But Parshuram never forgot Rudra, nor gave up on the prediction. It was his only shot at redemption. Parshuram had watched Kams's tyranny overrun all ethical boundaries, and lately, even more than before, his entire being ached for it to end.

Unable to continue the farce, he stepped out from the opulence of the palace and decided to walk through the spotless streets of Mathura. People turned to look at Parshuram, the venerable scientist, as they fluttered past on their winged shoes. Yes, Parshuram had invented these too. All around him now, humanity floated, unable to feel the ground beneath their feet. To be fair, there wasn't much left of Earth's surface; that was all long gone. Parshuram had worked to replicate the old natural world with a perfected new one – but to what end? Faux rivers, mountains and trees, model homes – all so perfect. A whirring sound of stasis echoed through the city as people clung to this pristine limbo.

Parshuram sighed and once again began punishing his mind with thoughts of the mistakes he had made. He had recast 'that day' innumerable times; yet, each time, it halted at the same place – it was the waiting for the saviour. It required extraordinary patience in the face of Kams's cruelty and killing. Each day, he convinced himself that this was the day the Messiah would arrive. Although lately, his conviction was beginning to flag. So he decided to have a straight-up one-on-one: *God – what's the plan? Do you even have one? Or is the universe just some randomness to you?* He waited for an answer; instead, he heard a din caused by the stage whispers inside Mathura. Groups assembled to talk about a rumour emerging from the dome's edge: 'Some people have been sighted.' The mere mention was enough to get the blood rushing through his veins again. Parshuram jumped into a hovercraft and made his way to the only other person in Mathura who believed.

Dr Yashoda was a gynaecologist, in charge of a hospital equipped to facilitate the safe birth of babies and keep mothers healthy. Only, Mathura no longer needed any of this since the monarch's ban on reproduction. So, Yashoda spent her days immersed in medical experiments and sports activities while trying to stay clear of Kams's random sexual partner radar.

Taller than most, her broad forehead, large eyes and sunken cheekbones were framed by short, brown, curly, wispy hair, but her most noteworthy feature was her erect posture. Yashoda had stopped ageing at forty-two, but she moved like a ballet dancer in her twenties, with her feet only gently tapping the ground as she walked. Her athletic build was in large part thanks to the hours she spent in sporting activity, her favourite being archery and swimming.

Dr Yashoda's dedication to a body that would not decay, no matter the abuse, was her denial of Mathura's status quo. She had watched Kams's army slaughter the wretched and worn sea of humanity, and every bone in her body ached with helplessness. To combat this pain, she conjured up death scenarios for Kams: *Maybe he will fall from a great height, which will smash his brains to a pulp*. She would then envisage the slow-motion version of his grey matter splattering … and an unknown wave of relief, like water over burning coals, would wash over her body. She savoured the vision of a mutilated, dead Kams, but ultimately the euphoria would subside and she'd have to face the facts. As of now, Kams was indestructible. After all, no one in the whole wide world could take him on. Primarily because the real wide world didn't really exist any more – he had destroyed it.

At this point in her mental reverie, she decided to have that straight-up conversation with the only entity she thought to be more powerful than Kams: *So, wherefore did the meek not inherit Earth?* She sat in her sterile, silent hospital room, not really waiting for an answer when she heard the hum of a hovercraft landing.

She leaned in to see what was being visited upon her now and sighed with relief. Ah, it was a co-believer.

Parshuram signalled to Yashoda to hop in. As they made their way across Mathura, they discussed the prospect of the new exodus. The rumour re-ignited a conversation they had stopped having. Yashoda was looking for reassurance. 'You think it's true?'

'Well, I am praying so very hard that it is.'

'Parshuram ...'

'Yes?'

'There have been so many of these, and he has killed them all.'

'I wish I could give up.'

Yashoda saw the pain in Parshuram's eyes. Once again, the realisation of Parshuram's predicament dawned upon her. His furrowed face contained the chronicle of every folly he felt he had committed, chief amongst them being trusting Kams.

Yashoda reached over and touched his arm. 'Come on, let's go. Maybe this time it'll be different.'

A turn later, she caught sight of them: the surging crowd hurtling towards the invisible, impenetrable barrier of the dome. 'There are so many ...' she murmured.

In the sea of humanity that was making its way towards Mathura, there could be the Messiah, the saviour, the person who would reverse Earth's destruction and, most of all, their bad decisions. Conflicted and anxious, they swung between hope and fear. Parshuram and Yashoda looked at each other with one shared thought: *He'll bring his army out, and that will be the end of it all.*

Chapter 3

The Messiah

Does dignity of life even exist? We've been fighting for it for decades and there were times it seemed within reach. As when there was a new leader. Or when the new laws were passed or that time when all world leaders came together. But the goalposts kept shifting – always placing fulfilment in the future. How much hope can one whip up? There is a point after which hope turns to desperation. Is today that point?

Outside the dome, Vasu's mind wandered as Devaki and he clung to each other as their defeated people transformed into a marauding horde. Moving with the force of a giant beast, they carpeted the expanse of the hill as they rushed towards the dome of Mathura. The air resounded with their voices: 'We are here!' 'This is the new world!' 'At last!' The cacophony of their gratitude sounded more like a war cry – a din that carried quickly through the barren expanse and crashed against the invisible dome. Mathura's bastion quivered with the noise of waning hope and cumulative desperation.

Vasu and Devaki squinted and saw something peculiar – as they suspected, there was a shimmering veneer, like a mirage that encased Mathura. The feeble light outside the dome reflected off its invisible surface, which seemed to ripple. Managing their expectations and breath, Vasu and Devaki moved forward with caution.

Inside Mathura, the events outside broke the lull. The period between the last exodus and this one had been long enough for its residents to be enthralled. Soldiers who polished their guns daily and used them primarily as hand rests now stirred like pythons uncoiling from hibernation. Hovercrafts came to a halt, and nervous voices replaced the hum of machines. The people of Kams's kingdom flitted about – confused and excited by this change of pace.

Kams lay akimbo on the bed, his thoughts so lost in a labyrinth that he no longer knew what they were. It was like a quicksand of overlapping, endless desires. Longings that were fulfilled a thousand times over and yet remained unquenched. His flaccidity had become a challenge for the others who occupied his bed. But he paid no heed and was now wandering down the streets of a fantasy where his bed was overflowing with ageing women, with bodies that had gracefully and without resistance succumbed to gravity; women with stark white hair, faces so artfully marked by age … and he imagined their crinkly skin pressed against his body. Fantasy resided in the land of the unattainable, and he felt something stirring. His sexual reverie was just setting sail when it was rudely anchored by the sounds of boots that rushed in unannounced.

Kams raised his head and felt a twinge of gratitude at the interruption. Any variation was now welcome. The other occupants of his bed missed not a beat and carried on with the drudgery of turning Kams on while the soldier addressed the king: 'Sir, I'm sorry to disturb you.'

'Well, now that you have, speak.'

'Your Highness, there are … are … Baharias – thousands, maybe hundreds of thousands of them. They are all rushing, sir … rushing towards Mathura.'

The soldier's words had an effect that Kams did not expect, but welcomed – he was flaccid no more! The whoop of joy from the people on the bed was as much a cry of relief as a celebration. Kams gazed down in wonderment at the turn of events. 'Tell me more.'

The monarch's request stumped the green-behind-the-ears soldier, but he carried on, determined to fulfil the supreme leader's command. 'Your Highness, they are hungry, thirsty and making lots of noise. They are … sir … they … sir … sick … sir. Also, some are walking, some running, stumbling, falling, some coughing … some, sir … sir … like garbage, sir. Your Highness, sir … your high … sir, just garbage…'

Kams waved his hand at the soldier to stop the gibberish. 'Tell them to follow the usual drill, and I will be with you shortly. Do not start without me!' His virility restored, Kams didn't want to hurry up. But he had to – after all, he had the important job of killing more pests seeking refuge. Better than sex, and less available.

Mathura was now all hurry-scurry. Teams in charge of the dome were fortifying it; the soldiers took position, while loudspeakers bellowed warnings to the rushing crowds outside: 'Do not come close to the dome, or you will be shot dead.'

Kams's court adjourned itself as the ministers made their way to a fortified war room. They stood there with multiple screens projecting the barely alive populace that was now their enemy. Brows furrowed and knuckles pressed into the table, they jabbed the screens pretending they needed a strategy.

Parshuram and Yashoda stood immobilised in the thrall of a large, desperate crowd. Here they were once again, with their fatigue, their hunger and their parched lips asking to be relieved, pleading for refuge. And yet, once again, neither Yashoda nor Parshuram could do a damn thing. Yashoda braced herself for what was to follow, but Parshuram was an eternal optimist, and so he scraped the barrel for the last resort. 'Why don't we appeal to Kams? Maybe, after all these years, he may have softened?'

'Right – so you mean the leopard must have changed his spots?'

Parshuram sighed, knowing that she was right, but he felt compelled to try. 'I'm going to talk to him. He does owe me, you know.'

Yashoda extended her arm to stop Parshuram from walking into a well of disappointment, but changed her mind when she realised he couldn't be dissuaded. He was going to take this last shot. She let him go and turned her attention to the surging crowd.

Yashoda scoured the group to see if her intuition might guide her towards what to do next.

Devaki and Vasu always lead by example. And so, they presumed that their values were well accepted – in fact, imbibed – by all in their country. Therefore, they considered the scrambling populace with some amount of dismay. The couple stood motionless as the crowds rushed forward, only to be stopped mercilessly by the invisible, pitiless dome. They threw themselves at it and fell like overripe fruit to the ground: gashed, oozing and reeling. Without delay, their mood swung back to despair. The crowd collapsed in a heap, lamenting their imminent demise.

The commanding officer was irritated by all the howling from a crowd that had minutes earlier flung themselves enthusiastically at the dome in a bid to enter Mathura illegally, and he hollered at his men: 'Go, ask the supreme commander to come. We are ready to start.'

Kams dressed for the occasion – the gold amulets, the blocks of emerald threaded into a necklace, a crown crusted casually with large diamonds, as if they had no value, but for the head they adorned. His loose silk pants and bespoke boots were all his body needed, because his chest had to stay bare to display his immortal masculinity.

He turned to his men and asked, 'Only two of you can accompany me; so please decide.' Kams smiled – his face clear of a grimace and mouth turned upwards in a smile. This rare occurrence triggered the audience on his bed; experience had taught them that this wide, almost manic grin was a signal to get away from what was coming. It made them fall into confusion, and they blurted – 'My legs are locked!' 'I have to wash my hair!' 'I just … you know … like, you know, like … literally can't!' And so on.

Kams raised his eyebrows, shrugged and took giant, quick strides towards his court. His mind was running the upcoming scenario on loop, which lent an extra spring to his step. Then, without warning, his pace was abruptly arrested. The upstanding, intolerably sweet like treacle – Parshuram – stood obstructing him. 'Ah, Parshuram … you heard?'

'Yes, there are so many, like the old days.'

Kams looked down at the diminutive man with the big brain and a droning voice, and bit back his anger and impatience: 'Yes, I have been informed.'

'They say this might be the last batch.'

Kams clenched his jaw, perfectly aware of where this conversation was headed, and knowing he could not stop the man from speaking the words he intended to utter.

'Kams, hear me out. We should save this lot. It would be such good karma. And … and … we need not give them the formula for immortality. So they will all die in time anyway. You see, it might be nice for us to be reminded of the circle of life – as it used to be.'

Something about what Parshuram said rang a distant bell in Kams's jaded mind. He was reminded of the ennui and how this could be a new variation – liberation from his overwhelming desires and finally freedom from the dreams that came true. He cautiously signalled him to continue.

Parshuram went on to hammer his point home. 'You know the circle that involves birth and death? We need not participate, but we can, you know, at least relive and remember what it was like?'

Parshuram lost Kams at the word 'birth'. The memory of Rudra's augury rose like a high tide and washed over his entire body, reminding him of what it felt like to be fearful and mortal. 'Parshuram, you know you are respected, but it's time you drew boundaries around your words lest they lead you to deep trouble.'

Parshuram had but one resort and he took it. 'Kams, you owe me – I gave you all you have.'

'And that's the problem – you already gave it to me. Now get out of my way.' And so, Kams brushed past Parshuram. His large frame leaning with aggression, he made forceful contact with Parshuram's comparatively smaller shoulder. In witness stood a large, empty courtroom that could afford hundreds to walk side by side without so much as sharing air. Kams knew it would destabilize Parshuram, and it did. The scientist's proud body stumbled. Deep within, he felt an upsurge of bubbling, seething anger. Its ferocity and swiftness surprised even him, and Parshuram caught it at the edge of his bristling skin, where he acknowledged that expressing his fury was simply not an option.

He thought about his living quarters. The large, grey, dilapidated structure made of canvas that stood on the outskirts of Mathura. The tent was his home and stood on a patch of the only dirt left in the city. Kams, and therefore all the others, concluded it was one of Parshuram's eccentricities to choose a flapping, discoloured structure instead of the opulent luxury available to every other resident. No one suspected that the tent was, in fact, a 'vaahan' or vehicle under construction. Such was Parshuram's conviction in the avatar's arrival that he had spent every waking moment planning for it. He had worked singularly to invent what would become the key to saving Mother Earth. But for it to work, it needed the avatar.

The swell of pain surged, took hold of Devaki, and seemed to spread around her like an orbit. Devaki was in labour, her baby was on its way but there was something extraordinary at play. While Devaki felt a pang of pain, the earth seemed to synchronously heave hard enough to shake the surface of the earth and rock the dome. It felt like an earthquake to announce the baby's readiness to be born. Unaccustomed to change and disruption, the residents of Mathura stopped for a moment, and everything stood still in the thrall of what they held in their vision – a large desperate populace that seemed lost and afraid except for the man and woman who were leading them, they seemed just startled. Devaki did not recognise the force controlling her, and she looked at her body as if it were a stranger. Her womb contracted in a final fierce spasm, and the water rushed forth – not a trickle but a rivulet that flowed past her legs, gushing with such ferocity that it parted the crowds as Moses might have the seas. It made its way through the dry dust, leaving a glistening trail in its wake. Devaki looked down at the deluge with as much surprise as Vasu.

Oblivious to these other-worldly happenings outside the dome, Kams strode into the enclosure that would be his podium to direct the massacre. He looked out over the arid expanse outside the dome and saw not people but termites crawling towards his precious sanctum, and simply said, 'Let's start.'

Bullets flew into a crowd that was, in any case, incapable of resisting. All they could do was to sink lower into the unrelenting hot dust. The pitiless bullets only served the purpose of grinding their skin and bones into the ground. Some of this blood from the massacre flowed and combined with Devaki's stream of placental fluid and became a sludge. It continued till it collided with the surface of Mathura's invisible dome and settled there, looking like maroon blotches suspended in the air.

Vasu looked on in horror as those he had led were mercilessly butchered. He uttered a war cry and leaned forward to rush to their defence when Devaki caught his arm in a firm grip. 'Vasu, Vasu, Vasu, save us, Vasu … save us.' Vasu had never heard his wife beseech him this way, but still had to think about his people. 'But what about them?' Devaki shook him with the meagre force she could summon to break him out of the self-defeating mission and propel him towards the one that they could yet win. 'We have to save this child, Vasu. We *must*.' He looked into Devaki's eyes and saw an urgent entreaty he did not recognise, but knew he had to obey. He gathered the last shreds of his strength, lifted Devaki on to his back, and wondered which way to go. And yet this apocalypse wasn't bigger than Devaki's instinct, and she pointed to a direction near the dome.

Dr Yashoda stood on the dome's edge, watching Kams's massacre in full swing. Her hands firmly clasped behind her back, swallowing tears that she had let flow on so many occasions before. Yashoda closed her eyes and did what she could – she prayed. Then, in the midst of the cacophony of death, a voice made its way into her aural landscape. It was the sound of a woman's voice pleading for help. It was only a quiet murmur – almost as if she may have been talking to herself. But it forced Yashoda to open her eyes and turn towards its source. Amongst the crowd of human beings fleeing from death was a pregnant woman – her skirt soaking wet, her swollen belly too large for her petite frame – perched on the back of a man who did not look like he had it in him to carry her. Yashoda marvelled at this sight of abject weakness and so much strength, and knew in her racing heart that what she saw was an exception.

Devaki looked at the purposeful woman encouraging them to follow her and was struck by how compassionate she seemed. Her eyes clung to Yashoda like a rock in a stormy sea, and she whispered in Vasu's ear: 'I think we will be fine, my love. I think we will be fine.' Vasu followed Devaki's pointing finger and noticed the woman who seemed to be interested in saving them.

Yashoda knew an access point reserved for doctors, and she hoped she remembered the code that had not been used in a long time. She breathed deeply and felt her hands assailed by a severe case of pins and needles. On the other side, Vasu and Devaki were leaning in exhaustion on the invisible surface that stood between them and clean air and watched Yashoda, their only hope, flailing her hands. They waited as she punched in the code. After a moment's reluctance, the door slid open.

Yashoda was aware that all breaches were monitored. There was surveillance everywhere, and there were those implants in the necks of all Mathura residents that tracked them. With no time to lose, she grabbed the dishevelled man and his wife and closed the door in one swift movement. 'Hello, my name is Yashoda. Please follow me. And try and walk by yourself or you will attract too much attention.'

Devaki slipped off Vasu's back, and another wave of searing pain made its way through her body. She gulped a mouthful of fresh air, and then another gulp and then another. The endless supply of oxygen made its way to her starved lungs and something stabilised within her. Devaki turned to Vasu as they gazed upon a fountain of water. Vasu wanted to feel lucky, but his guilt stopped him. The cackle of a now-unfamiliar sound mesmerised Vasu even as he tried to focus his tired, clouded eyes that stung from the realisation of the unfairness of it all.

Yashoda herded them forward to her hovercraft and said, 'Survival is a balancing act. One must take care of oneself while never forgetting that there are those who are less fortunate and need your help. But always after you have taken care of yourself first.'

The reminder served Vasu well when he spotted a small fortune of water bottles inside the vehicle. He pushed past remorse for abandoning his people and let his survival instinct kick in as he reached for what seemed like an elixir. He handed the first bottle to Devaki and then gingerly sipped the liquid, unsure how his parched body might accept the sudden bounty. It made its way into his body and cut through his oesophagus like a knife, while also washing it with relief. Devaki drained the water bottle and decided that now was a good time to do what she wanted to do all along – cry out in pain. A long, shrill cry prompted by the foetus trying to make its way down a canal clearly too small for it. Yashoda was startled. It was a sound she had not heard in a while, and reminded her of the human body's bad design. She said aloud: 'Why do humans have such bad body proportions? How is a baby that size supposed to make it out without this extreme pain?' No answers were forthcoming; just the sound of Devaki's howls of pain.

Existentialism. That wasn't a word that should have made its way to Kams's mind at the moment when so many lay strewn in blood and dirt, reiterating his complete hegemony over the globe. After all, moments like these were his raison d'etre. And still, the thought that he had breached all bastions of pleasure and power brought no joy. Had sadness defeated triumph? Had he built the wall just for himself? Who and what was he keeping out? His fear still resided right where he was.

Unbeknownst to him, a giant sigh escaped his lips. Too afraid to look it in the face, the military men stole glances in its direction, for it was a frightening sound to emerge from the fulcrum on which all this destruction rested. Kams felt the eyes on him and decided he needed a quick, swift and robust rebuttal. 'Get the forklifts out and remove the carcasses. We don't want the stench coming in here. Killing is fun but only until it starts stinking.' The laughter that followed was like the flora in Mathura – manufactured.

Yashoda had never been happier to turn on the lights of her unused operating theatre. Devaki and Vasu stood in the flood of hospital lights, feeling exposed and vulnerable. The spotless room left no space for failings. The cold metal surface of the operating table touched Devaki's little back, and she winced. Vasu grabbed a pile of surgical gowns and created a little buffer between Devaki's spine engulfed in waves of labour pain and the table. Her body was depleted and weak and he wondered if she could withstand the pain. Devaki read his thoughts, and she had to agree as she felt herself flagging.

Yashoda saw despair making its way in and held Devaki in an embrace: 'You're there … almost there. Push… push!'

Devaki nodded through clenched teeth as she put her entire might towards propelling the baby out. The waves of pain were only getting higher, and she felt defeated by their growing ebb. She turned to Vasu and felt alone in her pain. Was she the only one who had to bear it? 'This is awful … no one should have to suffer this pain.' Vasu stepped forward, hand extended but with no particular plan regarding what to do next. Devaki's infuriated expression was not providing any clues either. Yashoda stepped forward and took charge. It had been too long since she had done this, and she was sure as hell not going to share it. Devaki pushed harder as she felt sweat dripping off her brow despite the icy cold room. 'Take this damn thing out. Do something, aren't you a doctor?'

'We're almost there. Do this for the world, do it for humanity.'

Devaki shot a look of deep disgust at Yashoda at the thought of bearing this pain on behalf of a world that was clearly undeserving of being saved. Yashoda recoiled. She wondered how this contorted, angry woman could be giving birth to the one who would save Mother Earth. Wasn't giving birth to a messiah supposed to be an exalted act of self-sacrifice and forbearance?

Devaki had no interest in entertaining Yashoda's naivety while a creature was pushing against her uterine walls like an angry person swinging a bat. The waves of pain had crossed the line of unbearable. Vasu stroked her face and whispered with surety: 'Devaki, it will be over soon, and we will be parents. We made it so far, so this might be the one … the one that makes it!'

Devaki recognised that there was no going back, and she channelled her exhaustion, anger and deepest desire to be a mother and pushed as hard as she could. One final deep breath, and furrowed brows smoothened and arched in awe, the grimaces became smiles, and joy engulfed the room. Yashoda had seen more births than one, and it was always the same. A newly born life form consistently elevated those who witnessed its entry into the world.

After the euphoria had ebbed, Devaki sighed and lay back in the knowledge that her baby had left her womb and was now in the world. She wondered why there was surprise in Yashoda's voice when she announced, 'It's a girl.'

Devaki heard her gurgling before she saw her daughter. Propped on her elbow, she gazed upon Vasu holding the little girl that cooed at his touch. Was that a smile on the infant's lips? Weren't they supposed to cry? Devaki called out to her precious child: 'Hello, my little one. What's making you smile today?'

The newborn recognised the sound she had earlier heard while inside the womb and turned her eyes towards its source now. She took a deep breath that sounded like a gasp of joy, but there was still no wailing.

Devaki turned to Yashoda to confirm this wasn't odd, but found her preoccupied with something else.

'Krishna … is a girl! Our saviour is a girl! Such a delightful surprise!'

Yashoda's conjunction of the word 'saviour' with her child's name prompted her to take the baby back into her own hands. Devaki held her beautiful infant with glowing dark skin, flowing hair and those eyes – curious and staring wide – that seemed not of this world. Devaki's petite arms struggled to contain her large frame, and the infant's legs dangled from the turn of her mother's elbow. Devaki marvelled at the baby – her baby. The one who made it when the others before her succumbed to pollution, disease and war, even if it was at the expense of nearly tearing her in half. As if to compensate for the excruciating pain of birthing her, the baby raised her tiny hand and touched Devaki's cheek. In return, a tear made its way down her face and splashed on Krishna's little fingers. Vasu's heart welled with relief, and he encircled his family in his arms and squeezed just hard enough to prompt a laugh from his daughter. The sound, like her size, was much bigger than expected of someone who'd just made it out of the womb.

Yashoda decided it was time to call Parshuram, because sooner or later, this reverie would be broken – after all, they were still in Kams's Mathura.

Chapter 4

Death and Deathlessness

Goodness. Compassion. Equality. These lofty words trigger dreams in a world that lives and thrives in the nightmare of avarice, craving and longing. It would be less painful if idealism could be expunged and all could swim in the murky waters of hate and petty ambitions, but some suffer most for a vision only they hold. As if they have to pay for daring to imagine a better world.

Parshuram sat dwarfed by the screens that displayed the carnage of hope. Perhaps setting the tent ablaze would be the right way to celebrate this day of doom. To finally succumb to a lifestyle that he was responsible for creating. Honestly, how much had his moral spleen served him anyway? What had prompted him to stand with the losing side? And why did he choose the sinking ship instead of a buoyant life cruise? If he had any sense of practicality, he would join in the celebration of depravity in deathlessness. The very thought made him sob. Parshuram wiped his tears as he accepted that he had lost. He could take the immortality antidote and be set free from hanging on to a thread of a mere augury.

When his communication pod flashed Yashoda's name, he ignored it at first. But today, Yashoda was persistent, so he reluctantly tapped his wrist. Even through the hologram, the nervousness combined with excitement was palpable: 'Please come to the hospital immediately!' Yashoda raised her voice to drown out the clanging caused by the baby's new-found dexterity. The infant was playing with her ability to draw objects towards herself. Only a few hours into her powers, she wasn't well coordinated and was sending metal objects flying across the room. Parshuram watched this flurry in the background as Yashoda raised Krishna for him to see the source of the havoc. He looked at a little human being, writhing, giggling and drawing objects arbitrarily, dropping them and defying gravity as she lifted them off the ground again. With his eyes wide and mouth agape, Parshuram stared until Yashoda nudged him: 'Move, Parshuram, move, we have no time to lose. Get over here as quickly as you can.' Yashoda's voice broke the spell, and Parshuram started walking, but soon broke into a run.

Vasu and Devaki were not yet sure what these strange occurrences could mean. Their bewilderment compounded when Yashoda started talking about the prophecy. 'Parshuram will be here any moment. He will confirm that she is truly the Krishna, the saviour, the Messiah! You see, there was an augury that an infant would be born in Mathura. The infant will be called Krishna and will restore planet Earth, kill Kams and end his reign of terror and destruction. Kams – the one who snatched the title from the mighty Jamakhors by killing and defeating all of them. He who has captured mortality and has enslaved the world and its bounty. The regent of Mathura has but one nemesis – Krishna.'

Feeling intimidated by the colossal task assigned to her barely born infant, Devaki held her closer. Her soft skin nestled against her body, as if reassuring Devaki that she was indeed her daughter. And yet, something gnawed at her intuition. Her little daughter belonged not just to her but to the entire world. Moved by this thought, she held Krishna up, and Yashoda stroked her little forehead. The baby turned towards the caress and, freeing her little hand from Devaki's, she clasped Yashoda's finger. The touch triggered something that Yashoda had never felt before – the urge to protect and unconditionally love another being. Devaki saw this exchange and was assailed by both gratitude and a strong pang of jealousy. She quickly put Krishna to her breast and forced her into being the infant that she wanted.

She beamed with joy as Krishna set her adoring eyes on her source of food.

Parshuram burst in, breathing hard from the effort to contain his excitement and expectations. He rushed over to the infant, who lay in her mother's arms. 'How did you manage this, Yashoda? This is a miracle! And both of you are so very brave. Especially you as the mother to give birth against all odds – thank you! Can I hold her?' Something about Parshuram's kind eyes made Devaki feel secure enough to hand her child to him.

Parshuram lifted Krishna in the light and gazed at her as a jeweller would a diamond. He should have guessed that in an out-of-balance world that had tilted too far in favour of the masculine, the saviour would be a girl! He was reminded of the image of the fierce, dark goddess Kali straddling Shiva. Kali symbolising time, nature and mortality holds down Shiva, a parable for boundless space and sky. Without Kali, Shiva is limitless and headed for annihilation. For too long now, feminine nature – curbed, fettered and exploited was no longer available to control the marauding masculine throwing our world into chaos and confusion. The resolution was right there before him. A baby girl, born with supernatural strength and an augury that predicted her victory – this was nature's soldier. A wave of relief filled him – something he had not felt for decades. 'So, Krishna is a girl. It's official then – women are going to save the world!' Parshuram sensed both Yashoda and Devaki preening inwardly while Vasu's chest swelled with pride. But there wasn't any time to lose. 'We must move fast to my tent. It won't be long before they come looking for us,' he said.

The hovercraft made its way across Mathura to a patch of uninhabited land. Doubt played on everyone's faces as they sighted the ballooning tarp structure and wondered about its efficacy in keeping them safe. Inside, the tent was not a lot better than the outside. A small, neat bed; a modest table with chairs; and a large wooden chest made up all the furniture. The only apparent extravagance was the Persian carpet that covered the floor. However, the walls of the tent were most intriguing – apparently made of canvas, painted on them were scenes in the Indian miniature style of art. The pictures were bursting with colour: trees and animals animated with life, women and men dressed in finery that told of a time when the sun shone on flourishing fields and gardens, and gushing rivers generously provided for those on Earth. The people in these paintings looked on calmly through almond-shaped eyes that mimicked the form of a brushstroke. In sharp contrast to their physical appearance, the incidents that were depicted were scenes of destruction. These events from the history of the world showed detonated nuclear bombs, the slashing of forests, wars, and the killing of animals and humans en masse. These incidents had led to the destruction of the world and the corresponding rise of the Jamakhors. Prosaic events were transformed into poetry by the turn of some unknown artist's brush, but it still couldn't mask the horror of these incidents. Conflicted between dread and fascination, Devaki was enthralled by what she saw: 'These paintings look magical!' In agreement, the paintings transformed before their eyes and now depicted new scenes from other such events.

Although always changing, the scenes contained one person who remained constant – a young woman who was prominent in each work of art. She seemed to be present across time and space. A cluster of peacock feathers adorned her forehead, and a deep-blue–coloured body suit covered her body. She held what looked like a silver flute in her right hand and she looked in charge and at home, as if this was where she was born to be. They might have guessed her to be a superhero just by her body language, but none of them was entirely sure what these images meant, except for Parshuram. 'Do you recognise her?' His look of triumph conveyed to Devaki, Yashoda and Vasu that they were looking at Krishna in the future.

Parshuram spoke enthusiastically as he described his life's work. 'Amazing, this is the first time I am seeing her in these paintings. This tent is my biggest scientific accomplishment – it's my life's work and my leap of faith. Part of the augury that Rudra made was that the saviour would go back in time and right all the wrongs that led to the destruction of our precious Earth. And as she does this, with each altered moment in history, Kams will lose his power. And finally, he will … be finished.'

Yashoda understood Parshuram's scientific prowess, and she looked around, searching the tent for clues – 'And this tent will help?'

Parshuram smiled at being pre-empted. 'This tent is her vaahan, her carrier, and the paintings are portals into time. This tent, my dear friends, is a shape-shifting, intelligent being. It will grow as the saviour grows. It will do what all machines do – learn with each experience.' Realising that the others did not entirely comprehend what he said, Parshuram explained further: 'This tent is programmed to take Krishna to every event that she needs to circumvent, halt or change in any way. This tent will be her transport, her guide, her home and her protector.'

On the other side of Mathura, the death revelry had ceased, leaving a mass of blood and bones in its wake. A pulpy mess that was hard to scoop off the dusty, arid ground. They tried, nonetheless, and the revving engines and sounds of metal hitting rock carried into the dome and filled it with a sound that set most people's teeth on edge.

But Kams did not seem to mind at all. 'Suckers! Travelling all the way here just to die. They would have been better off dying right where they were.' Looking around himself, he noticed that his enthusiasm wasn't reciprocated with the usual ardour. In truth, the anticlimax was now beginning to wash over the soldiers. And Kams's oft-repeated 'cruelisms' no longer carried the same power. Feeling the loss of impact, he carried on in a bid to overcompensate: 'But if they hadn't come, we wouldn't have had the chance to remember how fortunate we are. After all, we are all there is of the human race, and no one – I repeat, no one – can ever kill us. So, I command you to celebrate in any which way you choose – all the resources of my kingdom are at your service.'

In return, he received a lacklustre cheer. Kams realised it would be a long and hard job to keep his subjects engaged with the business of eternity. His mind began to veer towards new schemes to keep them busy when he spotted the man from the surveillance team running in his direction. *Ah, there are more!* Kams thought gleefully. He was right. But not entirely.

'Sir … sir … sir … sir … sir…'

'Oh my god, man! What?'

'Sir, it seems there was a breach in the dome wall while we were killing … sorry, fighting off the intruders.'

'Details. Give us details, you imbecile.'

The man swallowed and tried to bring his nervousness to heel. 'A woman was … pregnant and … and it seems that the child was born in the hospital. Yashoda … helped, and Parshuram joined them, and they are now … they are in … in … in Parshuram's tent. The parents, Yashoda, Parshuram and … sir, dare I say.'

'Dare you don't say quickly enough.'

'The baby who could be … could be … could be … Kr … Krishna.'

No one dared utter that name in Mathura, much less in Kams's presence. Coming to think of it, he had not heard that name since the day Rudra said it; so he was not entirely sure that he had heard correctly. The confirmation came from a hum generated as every single neck of Kams's army strained and turned in unison to look at the man who dared to speak the name.

'And sir, I believe … I am told … it's a girl.'

While all of Mathura waited, Kams froze uncharacteristically – torn between the possibility of dying and the prospect of *finally* dying.

Chapter 5

The Escape

Newborns, no matter what species, are a marvel. They come with a clean slate and the possibility of an extraordinary life. Then there's vulnerability. It leaves us adults in charge, with the responsibility to turn clay into a thing of beauty. But my baby is different.

Devaki gazed down at her infant, and then at the mystical tent that was supposed to be her home, and wondered if she should be flattered or furious at being a mere cog in the cosmic plan. Krishna, her infant messiah, blissfully unaware, had fallen into a secure slumber. She took the moment to dissect her child's genetic inheritances. Krishna had got the skin translucence from her, and her dark skin harked back to her maternal grandmother. The woman was the stuff of legends because of her extraordinary physical strength. The tiny bud-like mouth was hers, and that prominent nose was an inheritance from Vasu's side of the family. The large, sagacious forehead was definitely from her beloved Vasu. Devaki felt a wave of love rising within her for her child with the perfect gene combination that helped her to survive while the others succumbed to pollution and disease. She kissed her forehead and decided that this child was the biggest compliment anyone had ever paid her.

Parshuram wanted this reverie to go on forever but knew it would not. 'We must prepare for … if … when Kams comes here.'

The thought of Kams coming for little Krishna sent a shiver down Yashoda's spine. 'We can run and hide in another part of Mathura.'

Parshuram looked at her sympathetically. 'You know both of us have trackers under our skin, right? And eyes are watching us everywhere. It's an infallible surveillance system.'

Yashoda wanted to believe there was an easy way out; she said, 'Maybe Vasu and Devaki can hide with the baby.'

Parshuram stated the obvious: 'For how long?'

Vasu shifted uncomfortably. These people were talking about his wife and child's future, and he had no real solution to offer. Had he walked all the way to Mathura to see them die at the hands of a tyrant? He looked at Parshuram's flailing hands as he pointed to a painting and wondered if he had any defence or help. But right before his eyes, he saw the shape-shifting image transform into a glowing tunnel, with no light at the end. Circular silver dust particles swirled at its periphery, making it look like a vortex in space. The sparkles of light swirled as if inviting them to step in and be carried away on their beams. Parshuram snapped his fingers as he called their attention to the task at hand. 'The portal will open only when the time is right. If Kams finds us, it will open, and we must jump in and take Krishna through this very gateway, this portal will carry her to safety. Krishna must be protected at all costs. The tent will take care of the rest.'

Devaki held Vasu's hand, and tears sprang to her eyes. She blinked them away and faced the fact that this child wouldn't be theirs for much longer. Vasu didn't need to turn towards Devaki to know how she was feeling. His stomach a cavity of sorrow and defeat, he accepted his inability to change the outcome. Vasu enfolded Devaki in his arms and momentarily felt whole again.

Prompted by Kams's pending arrival, Yashoda paced. Her mind raced and rebelled against thoughts of little Krishna's annihilation at the hands of the cruel king of Mathura. She stole glances at the portal and mentally planned her getaway moves. She counted the steps to the vortex and calculated the time it would take. Yashoda then positioned herself close to Krishna – ready and alert.

Just as Parshuram reached to part the flap of the tent to check the horizon for the regent's hovercraft, Kams's hand pre-empted him. He took hold of Parshuram's extended neck in one swift movement, held him in a vice-like grip and barked: 'Put him in chains.' Stunned by Kams's sudden arrival, Vasu had just enough time to stand up and shield Devaki and Krishna. With guns trained in their direction, Yashoda knew there was only one thing to do. She snatched Krishna out of her mother's lap and leapt into the portal. Devaki wailed as Yashoda turned to take one last look, and what Yashoda saw broke her heart. Kams left Krishna an orphan in one short moment. Kams used his sword and killed Devaki and Vasu as mercilessly as he had millions of others. Yashoda held on to Krishna so tight that the baby awoke. The first tears made their way down the infant's face as they hurtled through time.

Inside the tent, the paintings, now faced with danger, transformed like chameleons and disguised themselves as plain tarp. The soldiers chased after Yashoda and the infant but were confronted with nothing but blank, impassive canvasses. An enraged Kams and his army tore through the tent for clues and found nothing but proof of Parshuram's boring austerity. A soldier sensed the supreme leader's distress and made a helpful suggestion: 'Huzoor, should we torch the tent?' Kams knew a trick when he saw one, especially when it was created by Parshuram. They needed the tent and Parshuram to understand what was happening. There was also hope that, sooner rather than later, Yashoda's tracker would lead him to Krishna. And when he found that pesky infant, he would smash her small, soft head against hard rock and watch it splatter like a half-boiled egg … 'No – leave it be. Make sure that Parshuram stays alive … but barely.'

Kams stepped out of the tent and saw Parshuram shackled, bound and wincing. The feeling of having complete power over the scientist's fate rushed through his veins, making him ecstatic. 'Parshuram, Parshuram, Parshuram … now whatever are we going to do with you … and to you?' He slapped Parshuram with such force that the men around him feared he might have snapped the man's neck, but Parshuram's spine seemed to have grown a vertebra or two, and he turned to smile at Kams. Infuriated, Kams's brain began conjuring up ways to torture the man so that he could wipe that smirk off Parshuram's face. But soon everybody understood the reason for Parshuram's mirth. There, right before their eyes, the tent disappeared – like smoke in thin air! No drum roll, pomp or show – just one quiet whoosh and it was gone!

Kams looked around in shock at the vacated sandy plot and gritted his teeth as he spoke: 'Parshuram, don't celebrate just as yet. You're going to have a longer life than you wished for – much longer.'

Parshuram wanted to hold back, but the laughter sneaked past his survival instinct. It poured forth like a burst dam till tears rolled down his eyes. Gone were his restraint and subdued voice. This was the moment he had waited for his whole immortal life. 'Kams, the saviour is here! And she lives.'

Kams thought he saw the fleeting apparition of Rudra, the seer of his doom, making its way across Mathura's faux skies, leaving in its wake dread and agonizing anticipation.

Chapter 6

Ujwala

AD 2024
NORTHERN INDIA

If riches were counted not by what we possess but by what encompasses us, this is one helluva rich town. Mornings here make one a billionaire – one feels more fortunate than all others on Earth. There was only one thing to do – count one's blessings.

In the valley of gently rolling hills, a long road makes its way through an expanse of green meadows and fields of whistling elephant grass. Earlier that day, the rising sun had framed the little town of Ujwala with a halo. Now it had withdrawn the embellishment, blazed down, collided with the tarmac, and formed a mirage. The sounds of stirring and revving filled the usually quiet air as black soot rose from machines that paved the way for Ujwala's development.

Most recently, this hamlet had been mapped and was raising considerable interest. This map revealed a large field, at the end of which was a ramshackle structure that housed the local government school. About a five-minute walk away flowed a glistening river, and by it lived Satya, a thirty-two-year-old man who kept bees that made sweet honey.

Satya was a man thrust out by the forever-churning urban mill. Tired of the lack of tenderness, he picked up his belongings, said goodbye to his trepidations and made his way to the mountains. He wandered and found a valley and, within it, untouched Ujwala. Here, he settled into such contentment that he thought he might never leave.

Today, Satya was contemplating his wealth – a river in his backyard, a lush field for a garden and majestic mountains overlooking his home and bee yard. As the eggs sputtered on the frying pan, he was reminded of the only person he missed. His mother spent all her days over a burner, conjuring up meals for his wealthy father, who could hire a gourmet chef or two but insisted that his wife be the one to do the job. It was an unpaid position and, as time passed, also turned into a thankless one. She withdrew into a stoic silence. She gathered her love for nature, her wanderlust and sprinkled that desire with the spices into slowly simmering curries. With every turn of the ladle, she wandered further and further away. Since he could remember, Satya ingested these longings with the morsels that made their way from his mouth to his stomach and then his bloodstream. Satya flipped the perfect Spanish omelette off the pan and on to his plate. He ate as he smiled at the memory of his bilocating mother, who wandered even as she seemed stationary.

Satya made his way to his favourite creatures. His joy knew no bounds as the beehives were laden, and the bees were buzzing around his masked face celebrating all the work done. That was until the helicopters broke the spell with their noisy rotors. There were two, and they were making their way to the town square. It was an exalted title for an area that consisted of eight shops, one restaurant and a chapel that was a colonial hand-me-down. The stained-glass windows, the high ceilings and wooden benches were crafted a century ago, and not much had changed since. The choppers chose the grounds near it to make a landing, raising dust and the hackles of those who had come to expect that nothing would ever change in Ujwala.

Ten-year-old Eka sat in her home on the first floor of an old structure made of mud and wood. The interior of the house stood in stark contrast to its exterior and was overflowing with shiny new objects. The front room was dominated by an LED screen that eclipsed the wall and was currently blaring a soap opera. Eka watched curiously – a woman cried, a man shouted, an old lady quivered, and some others looked shocked – repeatedly. Unable to understand the lure of these dramas, Eka turned to her mother, Priya Mehra. Petite Priya's brown eyes were riveted to the events on screen, while Yash Mehra's shining dark eyes were inspecting Eka's half-eaten breakfast. 'Eat up, child – you will be late for school.'

At the mere mention of school, Eka pushed her plate away. Priya distractedly reached out and slathered her face with cream that promised lighter skin. Eka squeezed her eyes shut and waited for it to be over so she could wash it off. You see, Eka seemed pliant, but she did as she pleased.

In another home quite different from Eka's, Atmaram Gupta – a man in his seventies, his back slightly bent, spectacles glistening – was watering his plants with a small watering can, to avoid over-watering them. His loving care was apparent in the flourishing flora that crowded the large courtyard of his home. Rahul, his nine-year-old grandson with his perfectly combed hair and neatly creased uniform, was cautiously tiptoeing around this potential mud-stain minefield. Atmaram smiled at his guarded grandson – 'Rahul, my sweet child, see, like a person, each plant needs individual care.'

'How, Dada?'

'See how you and each of your friends are different. If I speak loudly to you, what will you do? You will be sad. But to Rumi and Dhwani, you can raise your volume as high as you want, and they will simply laugh.'

No sooner had he uttered their names than Dhwani and Rumi appeared like unsummoned genies. They had surprising stealth for children with no volume control. These twelve-year-old twins were identical only in personality – Rumi, a stocky, strong boy and Dhwani, a tall, lanky girl who liked to lean on objects whenever possible. The arrival of his two torrential classmates worried Rahul because, at the other end of the courtyard, Rahul's parents considered them with disapproving eyes.

Rahul's father, Vijendra Gupta, was a tall man, usually dressed in a white cotton kurta with Gandhi glasses framing his eyes. But his life philosophy had as much in common with Mahatma Gandhi as fish with the golden sands of the Thar Desert. Vijendra was like a jigsaw puzzle in search of its missing pieces. His wife, Veena Gupta, was perforce at fault for this lost and never-found mission. Consequently, her face was perpetually set in a grimace that obscured her natural beauty.

Rumi and Dhwani scanned the room with their eyes, took a collective decision to turn their backs on the 'dissatisfieds', and spoke simultaneously to Atmaram.

'Hello, hero!' Dhwani said while resting her lean frame on Atmaram's arm. This daily interaction never failed to make him smile. 'Cool cool plants you got there,' she said. And like every other day, something about this casual bonhomie irked Vijendra Gupta. 'Baba, you come inside, please. You'll catch a chill and then it'll be a big pain for us.'

This tone of voice raised the hackles of the under-thirteens crowded around Atmaram and to stem a rebellion, he hastily made his way into the house.

Rahul was crestfallen, and Dhwani felt her friend's pain. She leaned in, encircled him in a huge hug, and whispered: 'Let's go!'

Rumi, Dhwani and Rahul sprinting through the streets of Ujwala were no novel sight, nor was Rumi leaving marks in the mud as he trailed a stick behind him.

A few turns later, they arrived at the door of Rumi and Dhwani's house. Rabia, the mother of the twins, waited at the door of their home. She knew the dual storm was about to return at any moment as they had rushed out without carrying the package for their father. She had the patience of a woman who became a mother later than most. She and her husband Amir had spent a considerable part of their lives buried in books of poetry and philosophy. Soon, their lives took on the same meter.

Consequently, Rumi and Dhwani's birth was delayed – by the standards of societal expectations – but for Rabia and Amir, the twins appeared right on time.

'Oh stop, stop, stop. Listen, give this to your father at the shop on your way to school.' Rumi was in full throttle and couldn't be stopped. 'Okay, Mother! Now mooooooooooooove.'

They ran on as they tossed the packet. Rahul, who feared the outcome of a missed catch, decided to have no part in it. Instead, he raced ahead and waited safely inside Amir Hussain's shop. In the shop, Rahul marvelled at the knick-knacks – carpets, lamps, clocks, salt and pepper holders, toys and handmade paper diaries. Amir and Rabia Hussain curated and shared their choices with their customers. They travelled and collected items, buying two of every object – one for their home and the other for the shop.

Rahul stared in admiration at a particular toy wooden cart that was too intricate to be a toy. The camel drawing the cart seemed so real that his imagination leapt on to the back for a ride and then Dhwani burst in and tossed the packet to Amir, who caught it like a practised catcher. 'Rumi and Dhwani, can you go slow and do things as they are meant to be done?'

Dhwani answered, 'Of course not.'

'I thought as much – off you go.'

The children moved swiftly till the machine spouting bellows of dark smoke halted them. They watched in fascination as tar trickled on to the road. The black gooey material dripping on to the old dusty track fascinated Rumi, and he stepped straight into it and jumped on to the mud nearby. He alternated a few times till he thought his shoes were unbreakable. Nothing like gooey tar and mud to create a thick layer under his shoes, like another sole for this footwear but he couldn't revel too long in his fortified shoes because Rahul and Dhwani had already sped ahead.

Being surrounded by tall elephant grass always led to the 'lost in a jungle' game. Rahul, Rumi and Dhwani conjured up wild beasts, bad weather and monsters as they raced through. Their collective imaginations created more horror than was necessary for an early morning run to school.

Rahul was the first to spot the beast. 'Watch out, there is a lion coming after us!' Dhwani became its prey. '*Oh my god!* The lion bit my hand.' Naturally, Rumi was fascinated by the imaginary gaping wounds: 'So much blood.'

'Run, run, run ...'

Pretend panic kicked in, and there was scampering, falling and stumbling till they emerged from the field and ran straight into Jeet.

Jeet was fifteen years old, the eldest, the tallest and the declared leader of this pack. His piercing eyes and fierce, warrior-like posture made it clear that he took this position seriously. Eka stood by his side and smiled widely at her friends. Jeet's well-chiselled face was stern and disapproving. Arms crossed, he looked down at the little ones: 'So? Why are you late? If Eka here can make it on time, why not you?' Jeet bent down and pointed his finger straight at Rahul, who wilted. Eka swiftly took hold of Jeet's finger and forced it down while giving him a disapproving look. 'Haha, Jeet, very funny. Stop scaring them. Let's go now.' Jeet had no intention of scaring anyone, and to compensate, he broke into a wide smile combined with some face-pulling. The response was laughter, and together they walked towards their school's semi-constructed building.

Below a cracked blackboard, Ravi Sharma, a man in his thirties and the sole teacher at the Ujwala Government School, was sitting on a chair with his legs stretched on the table, reading a three-day-old newspaper because he did not give much credence to time. This served the children of Ujwala well because they were constantly and consistently late. Getting their group together was akin to weighing frogs; getting them in one place was no easy task.

A gentle breeze, unobstructed by the half-constructed walls, brought the smell of sweet grass. A friendly goat ambled through the single classroom. The children waited for the animal to make its way through and found seats for themselves. Although of various ages, they learnt their lessons together. Rumi and Dhwani, tired of the languid pace, sneezed loudly and in unison. This startled their teacher Ravi Sharma and served to attract his attention.

'Please sit down and open your books. Now be quiet because this is a school, not a meadow.' Ravi Sharma said this while pointing to the pasture, with the tall grass waving back at him. The children, now used to this unintended irony, sighed and opened the books of their choice. Ravi Sharma then lifted his hand and waved in no particular direction. 'Jeet, come here and take over the class.' Jeet shook his head in resignation at what was an almost daily occurrence. Eka rolled her eyes with such ferocity that it seemed like her eyeballs might shoot out and strike the teacher dead. She decided that someone needed to have words with the errant teacher, 'I suppose you're going to go out again, sir?'

'You think I am only your *teacher*? I have other important work, like election duty for the government.'

'Last week also you had some duty. Who will teach us?'

'Last week it was vaccination duty … but you won't understand because you are small – small, small, small. Tiny little things with tiny little brains.'

And with those well-thought-through, profound words – Ravi Sharma picked up no belongings that he hadn't brought and exited the classroom.

A goat chewed on the bush that lined the boundary of the school. She munched sanguinely. No thought crossed her still mind; only the intention to ingest and digest … till Rumi and Dhwani decided to fill her ears with words to pass the time in the now-open period that lay ahead of them. They had taken each ear and were putting their persuasion skills to work. Rumi tried encouraging the animal: 'Say, "I'm a goat."' Dhwani thought it was ridiculous to set unattainable goals for the goat. 'Rumi, don't be silly. That's too hard for a goat to say. Just say "goat",' she stage-whispered straight down the aural passages of the animal.

Jeet and Eka made their way up the branch of a tree and sat with their legs dangling, invested in the outcome of this endeavour. Rahul watched, breath bated but sceptical, to see if they would succeed.

The goat continued to chew as she reflected upon Rumi's and Dhwani's words. She shook her head, clearing her mind, drew a breath in the way of a snort and paused before standing up and bleating. The sound was much louder than usual, as if rebelling against human snobbery that imagines that the only language worth speaking is theirs. To drive her point home, she wandered through the empty classroom, dropping on the way the outcome of the chewing. Then she exited, leaving them once again with nothing to do.

Eka was the first to see that this game was over. 'Let's go to play!' Her words acted like a lever that pushed everyone to sprint. There they were, the midday sun shining upon them, running through a lush field, their laughter fused with the cool breeze, the grass grazing their legs, and life seemed perfect at that moment.

On the other side of Ujwala, the coloured patterns from the stained glass were getting shorter on the chapel's gleaming floors as the light outside moved away from the horizon. The passengers of the helicopters that had earlier disturbed Satya's bees now sat on wooden benches doing what they were not used to – waiting. Mukesh Mehta, popularly known as MM, was accompanied by two people called 'The Lackeys' for obvious reasons. MM was expecting a crowded room full of people eager to trade their boring, idyllic lives for money. Instead, he found an empty church. This set off his ferocious leg shake that made the stolid bench vibrate and lead to The Lackeys rocking to the rhythm of his impatience. 'Call that idiot Vijendra Gupta – where is he? And where are all the people?'

Eventually, they ambled in. Unmindful of MM's impatience, they discussed the weather and exchanged the minute details of their lives. What did they eat for breakfast? Was it too warm for this time of the year? Were the rose bushes forming buds? And then there was the discussion on digestion, which got more complicated. You see, in Ujwala, they had all the time in the world.

To speed things up – The Lackeys rigged up a screen at the altar. It stood directly under the cross with an uncannily real-looking, martyred Jesus appended to it. It was a compliment to its creator that it seemed like, at any moment, the blood from the Son of God's hands and feet would make its way down on to the screen. The strangeness of this positioning was not lost on the audience as they peered curiously to see what would happen next. No doubt this further annoyed an increasingly restless MM: 'Pull the screen forward, you brainless fools.'

The townspeople had gathered here for what was said to be an 'urgent matter', and watched MM's moves with some interest. Many had come spurred only by the unusual occurrence of two helicopters flying over Ujwala. It was almost a full quorum that included Amir and Rabia Hussain, the parents of precious Rumi and Dhwani; Jeet's grandfather Devendra Singh Rathore – a man with the handlebar moustache characteristic of a former military man; Rahul's grandfather Atmaram Gupta; and Eka's parents Yash and Priya Mehra.

Vijendra Gupta believed he was unique and above others in some way. It constantly amazed him that no one else around him saw that. He was and never would be, just another person in Ujwala. Something huge awaited him, and he was going to seize the opportunity when it presented itself. Accordingly, he had taken the important seat right beside MM. Buoyed by this position, he spoke with newly acquired authority: 'We have here with us the owner of the famous Wholly Treat Foods Inc … WTF for short. Mr Mukesh Mehta!'

Before he could continue his eulogy, it was truncated by the loud sound of the creaking door opening at a languid pace. Satya wasn't known for his excellent timing; so no one else was surprised when he made a noisy entry and stood silhouetted against the midday sun, his long shadow falling on MM and Vijendra Gupta. They wanted to step out of the shade cast by Satya, but were firmly hemmed in by the loyal Lackeys. MM raised his eyebrows at Vijendra Gupta, seeking an explanation; so he introduced him: 'This is Satya. He lives near the meadow and is a bee-keeper … that's his full-time job! Yes, come in quickly, please … and grab a seat. We're just about to begin.'

Mukesh Mehta stepped forward to start the business of preaching to what he presumed was the choir. The Lackeys stood like decorative figurines, framing him on either side. MM furrowed his brow, ignored their presence and turned on an overhead projector with a click. The light flickered and images of Ujwala came alive. MM had specially hired the designers of The Grand Auto Theft to bring the town to life, complete with its fancy, foreign-looking streets, American characters and even some quick car chases. You see, it was MM's favourite game, and he spent hours of his free moments with it. But, judging by the audience's puzzled reaction, perhaps *they* did not. He decided to barrel on regardless: 'We are proposing a complete change, and a brand new and improved Ujwala, just a few kilometres away.'

A hum of discomfort met the whirring of the machine as Ujwala faded to black and MM spoke enthusiastically: 'I present to you, Ujwala Again! We will build a whole new town for you.' With these words, right before their eyes, they saw the wild, untamed, messy, defiant nature of Ujwala morph into the docility of a concrete, blemish-less, perfect little world with more than one shining glass building in its midst. Opaque concrete structures appeared to devour all that they towered over without so much as reflecting upon it. A wave of shock passed through a hall dappled with stained glass shadows. Spots of blue, green, red and yellow rippled as those seated turned to look at each other for confirmation. *Does everyone feel the same way*, asked their darting eyes. Some seemed shaken, some intrigued, and others looked as if they'd just been invaded. But these were the reactions of those who were uninitiated to the crusaders of 'development'. Satya, who had recently moved from the city to the innocence of the small town, knew the marauders of the material world, and was irritated by this turn of events.

Mukesh Mehta was not accustomed to reading a room; so he carried on unhindered: 'Of course, there will be shops for antiques and baskets and all other local things. *Free!* It will be full of all modern conveniences and much more money.' He said the word 'money' with an action that looked like he was flipping an invisible coin.

Satya bent his head backwards as he reeled with deja vu. He knew this spiel and understood where it was headed. 'Free? I don't think so. You represent a big and profitable company and so I can't see you doing anything for *free*.'

Satya's words set off MM's twitches as his right eye started to flutter – he hated when that happened. He never understood why people didn't just buckle before money; after all, it was the only real thing in the world. Vijendra Gupta saw with some rising panic how MM was devolving into one big tic, and spoke louder than he intended: 'One should believe in people's goodness, you know. Why be cynical and think the worst of people? We should think positive and not be negative.'

Satya drew on some reserves of calm that he had shored up in Ujwala and spoke in a measured and deliberate manner: 'As a matter of fact, I do believe in goodness, but not in *his*.' As he said this, he pointed right at MM. Surprised at seeing Satya's index finger extended in his direction, MM's stomach lurched, and the twitch spread to his forearm, which now looked to the onlookers like he was lifting an invisible weight. He was worried that the spasm could make its way to his leg and turn him into a low-level Elvis impersonator. Mukesh Mehta pointed towards the lush field. 'Ujwala is a small town with a large meadow. We will build a state-of-the-art factory that will make … make will, making … willing … simple simple potato chips.'

Satya said aloud what he was thinking: 'What utter nonsense!'

With this, the spasm found a new route to MM's shoulders and forced his neck to turn from side to side to contain it. Ex-general and Jeet's grandfather Devendra Singh Rathore stared at MM with one side of his mouth lifted in an awkward expression of wonder.

Mukesh Mehta spoke hurriedly before things deteriorated further. 'Oh, I forgot to add … We will also be allocating a nice space for Mr Satya so he can display his honey or whatever.'

'Go to hell. I'll never trade the field and this town for anything.'

Yash Mehra had made an art out of sitting on the fence. It was usually a comfortable position to act as if he was in the centre, but something about Satya's tone tipped him over. 'This should be a decision made by the residents of this town, not recent entrants.'

Used to having fingers pointed at him, Satya spoke evenly: 'Does this town belong to you?'

A chapel constructed to carry the voices of people all the way to God amplified the decibels. Soon, arguments were elevated to slanging matches as insults reverberated and words pierced hearts.

Mukesh Mehta watched in horror as this open conflict assailed his body. In response, he retrieved his expensive smartphone and dialled, hoping to convey that he was an important man with so much to do. It didn't deter the voices from rising; so he made his way out of the chapel as quickly as possible. The Lackeys trailed behind him like the courtiers of a tiny estate.

The residents missed every single cue, including MM's hurried exit, absorbed as they were in being polarised in their views. It was old versus new, nature versus development, and mostly about whether one should throw the baby out with the bathwater or not.

Amir Hussain watched the exchange of insults between the residents of a town that prided itself in its ability to accept differences. Before his eyes, he saw a tear appearing in the delicate fabric of diversity that the elders of Ujwala had woven with such love and care. He was crestfallen at being unable to stop this discord that was playing out right in front of his eyes.

However, about a hundred kilometres above Earth, there was just the silent humming of gravitational waves. Things seem different when one is looking down from overhead. Known as the 'overview effect', the distance and vantage point provides a broader perspective. Buzz Aldrin, the astronaut who saw the earth for the first time from space, described it as a 'brilliant jewel in the black velvet sky', while for those living on the rock, it was just dust, dirt, strife, and a yearning for peace. Like the musk deer, they looked outside for what was theirs all along.

Chapter 7

Arrival

The lingering missing is a real thing. Those who carry it know it is as tangible as a childhood toy. It becomes a part of one's emotional vocabulary when leaving is a lifestyle. Arrival, departure, arrival, departure – the never-ending cycle of living between the poles of anticipation was one of the challenging parts of being 'The Saviour'.

The townspeople emerged from the chapel as the sun began its descent towards the horizon. Discord is indeed a time-consuming business. Some whispered their fears and apprehensions, while others shared their hope for a new way of life.

Unable to contemplate the eventuality of losing his island of peace, Satya walked alone through the field and listened to the sounds of impending nightfall. The chirping of birds gave way to the cacophony of crickets; stroked by the wind, the grass rustled and the trees whistled a lullaby. The sky unapologetically flaunted its array of stars. Satya paused in front of the river that reflected these nocturnal lights and shadows. The sigh that escaped him was not one of resignation but of the recognition of the long fight ahead. He wondered if the citizens of Ujwala were equipped to take on the might of corporate greed and systemic corruption. As the swirling thoughts began to pick up speed, Satya chose to sleep. Before slumber claimed him, a last arbitrary one arose from his Jenga of ideas: *Saviour stories are such lies*. And then he fell into a dreamless sleep.

****

The tent indicated when it was nearing a destination. The change in its behaviour was imperceptible but evident if one was paying attention. It took on a sterner posture, as if bracing for something.

Krishna stretched her twenty-five-year-old, rather tall body and marvelled at how her four-poster bed never shook when the tent moved. Yet, when the indication came, she knew. Krishna loved the tent. It had been a friend, compatriot and even a parent to her. However, its hallowed architect Parshuram could have gone a step further and programmed it to provide complete information, like where they were heading or what time period it was. She had never met Parshuram, and made a mental note to bring it to his attention when she did.

Krishna changed into something presentable. Not knowing the time period did not exactly make her a fashionista, but these were not her concerns.

On Earth's surface, deer grazed on succulent green grass under the moonlight. Nibbling fussily, they whispered that something was different. It wasn't a scent they knew or a sound they recognised. A fawn was convinced there was magic in the air. Right about then, a giant creature dropped out of the darkness, rushed towards the field and scared the herd nearly to death. They ran with a heart-attack–inducing ferocity and watched from behind the trees as the creature appeared on the field. A mother deer pushed her curious fawn behind her as she strained to make sense of what she was looking at. It landed in a crumple and then seemed to grow before their eyes. As it expanded, it didn't look like a creature but more like a house. Then, like a chameleon, it changed colour from a dowdy brown to a red so bright, it could have been a rose in full bloom. In the glistening moonlight, a tall human emerged. She walked unsteadily, as if she were a baby finding her steps. Then, without warning, she flew up like a bird. Now they had seen enough, and the herd fled with the resolve to never return.

Krishna turned to look in the direction of the bolting animals and wondered what was causing them to hurry away. The unusual nature of the situation had not yet occurred to her because she was preoccupied with gravity. The goddamn pull was different everywhere in the universe, and it always took her a moment or two to recalibrate. Being in the air was easier. Krishna looked out at the expanse of Ujwala and felt a mixture of excitement and trepidation. It was her first mission, and she had waited for it her whole life. She said aloud, 'What year is this?' The question drew the rest of her crew out of the tent. And one by one, they emerged – a freak show of saviours.

Anita, the lithe transgender, preferred the pronoun 'she'. Her skin bleached beyond pigmentation, it had a sheen as if she were wearing a latex body suit. Her short, raven-dark hair framed her delicate face. Although in her twenties, her eyes had the weariness of someone who had lived a century too long. Anita bent down to touch the grass and felt a wave of exhilaration go through her body – *This is going to be good.*

Maya admired Anita's tenderness, for she herself had a hard time summoning up compassion. Maya was rumoured to be in her forties, but there was nothing in her appearance that made her age apparent. Her dark skin, strong bone structure and solid build made her a force to reckon with. Like Anita, Maya's expression was marked by impassivity. She wore a scarf over her long unruly hair, and her ankle-length skirt flapped in the wind as she sniffed it to tell the year: 'It's … 2024.'

It took Ryan longer to make his way out of the tent. The exit was too small for his tall frame, so he waited patiently for the tent to expand and make space for him to come through. Ryan was strong – superhumanly strong. He was a people pleaser and smiled more than he needed or even wanted to. It's a different matter that the beaming happened nine feet above the ground and was not visible to most. Today, Ryan heaved with laughter as he celebrated being back. 'Oh well, we're back on Earth!'

Prince, although a dwarf, had a persona larger than Ryan's. His confidence flew higher than Krishna's, and no matter the situation, he always knew his way out. Plus, he was not entirely unaware that his pert nose, shoulder-length hair and angular face with sharp eyes made him a good-looking man. 'We are here, and we will get this done … although what it is we're doing … is that clear to anyone yet?'

Back on the ground, Krishna frowned, closed one eye and tried to concentrate, hoping against hope that there would be an answer. Her intuition could glean only the magnitude of the adventure but not its nature. 'We better get a good night's sleep. I have a feeling 2024 was a big year – for sweet Mother Earth and for us.'

Chapter 8

The Mission

Peace, like a still pond, was disturbed by the smallest pebble, leaving ripples that go on and on and on. All it took was one tiny, minuscule drop of dissatisfaction to set off a tidal wave of fragmentation.

Amir Hussain was worried about Ujwala. Named after the local goddess, the deity of light, Ujwala was used to being bright, sunny and bountiful, with mostly satisfied residents. It was, therefore, with some dismay that he saw its sangfroid crumbling. Hours after MM's departure, the arguments still raged. This morning, S.D. Rathore and Vijendra Gupta gathered with Amir Hussain in his shop. The morning light streamed, with its particles dancing through the glass door of the shop's entrance. These beautifully arranged specks surrounded the group huddled near the rack of sundry toys.

Amir tried to convince them of what was necessary: 'You see, money is not everything.'

It wasn't all that surprising that Vijendra Gupta didn't buy it: 'That is your opinion.'

Rathore, a military man, would not go down without a fight. 'Yes, but it's an opinion worth considering.'

Vijendra Gupta retorted, 'Yours is the thinking of old-timers.'

Amir Hussain watched nervously as voices and bile rose. He welcomed his children's bad manners with relief for the first time. Dhwani and Rumi burst into the shop and sent the Buddhist gong flying while instantly disassociating themselves from the catastrophe by gazing upon the fallen object with surprise. Faces flushed, they waited for the endless echo to recede before they spoke. Dhwani was the first to go: 'Abbu, you won't believe it!'

Now Amir loved his children – every part of them – even their sometimes-vivid imagination. 'I will believe anything both of you come up with,' he said. Rumi continued, 'A huge tent is sitting on the field.' It was too much of a stretch even for Amir, and he replied, 'Oh! So it's sitting, not standing?' Amir Hussain and Vijendra Gupta erupted with laughter at what they thought was a clever retort. Septuagenarian D.S. Rathore searched for the humour but eventually shook his head and gave up. Even for him, this was a joke only his dad would get. To echo that sentiment, Rumi and Dhwani sighed in exasperation. Dhwani continued, 'No, really, it's no joke – it's magnificent! Red, gilded, beautiful and so big. It's hard to explain, Abbu.'

'It's true – I swear.' Rumi said, pinching the skin on his throat with his thumb and index finger. The earnestness of the gesture made Amir think that perhaps they were speaking the truth.

In another part of Ujwala, Krishna emerged from her tent and stretched cautiously, her mind rifling through options to stabilize and overcome the gravity hurdle; she gazed down at her non-cooperative feet and decided the best option was to go slow. Maya – perched on Ryan's shoulders, trying to fix a sign atop the circus – watched as Krishna tiptoed in a bid to gratify Earth's gravity: 'Go on, it isn't all that bad.' Encouraged by her, Krishna stepped forward confidently. A second too late, she understood it was a bad idea. In free fall and headed for the ground, she used her superpowers and stopped with just centimetres to spare – 'Oh goddammit! You can do the setting up. I'm going to sit this one out.' Prince was getting tired of the gravity excuse already, and there was still a lot to be done. 'Sure, but you can still help.' Saying this, he set down a stool and placed a basin full of potatoes submerged in water in front of Krishna. With a flourish reserved for the exalted, he handed her a peeler.

Krishna looked at him through her large, dark eyes and shook her head. She hated getting her hands wet, and despised peeling.

She decided there were no trivial reasons to use one's superpowers and set about holding the peeler in the vicinity of the vegetable while it peeled itself. Anita noticed – 'Krishna, you are so very lazy.' She contemplated a fitting response when the grass in the field rustled as if heralding the arrival of a creature. She stopped, her breathing slowed, and her eyes squinted, trying to gauge the danger. Krishna could feel her team straining in the same way as they attempted to discern the raised, unintelligible voices. With some sense of anticlimax, she resumed the mock spud peeling as she realised that the creatures concealed in the shrubbery were just humans.

Behind the grass, the residents of Ujwala were inching towards the red gilded structure with trepidation. Fear made them crouch behind the elephant grass, making full-grown men look like beasts on the prowl. Perhaps the most doubled over was Mukesh Mehta who, spurred by the fear of his boss, had rushed to Ujwala as soon as he heard the news. Folded over with anxiety, and sans caffeine and no morning ablutions, his gut and head throbbed with a dull pain.

For the children of Ujwala, this was an exciting moment. They finally had a resident circus and were getting impatient with the tortoise-like pace. Rahul, the dutiful son of Vijendra Gupta, felt a twinge of pride for what he presumed was his father's doing: 'It's beautiful, Papa. Nice circus you put here. Thank you.' This strangely offended Vijendra Gupta: 'Don't talk gibberish. We haven't set up any circus.' Impatient and fed up, Satya decided that the only way to know for sure was to walk straight to the tent. So he was the first to see it.

In the middle of the field stood a gigantic, gilded tent in an other-worldly shade of red, bound down with copper-coloured ropes; white shimmering ribbons adorned its crown. On top was something between a skylight and a latticed window that looked delicately carved from stone but was pliant fabric swaying in the breeze. The tent glowed from within, giving it a warm halo. Headlining it was a board with multicoloured bulbs that announced this was 'Krishna Circus'.

Satya's abrupt halt meant that the others collided and froze like they were in a game of 'Statue', suspended in mid-movement by what stood before them. The children did not even bother to close their awestruck mouths. In response to the gob-smacked audience, the tent displayed its final flourish as the lights flashed and the ribbons fluttered with a new ferocity. Krishna looked at the expressions of the motley bunch and knew that the tent was doing its usual careening and preening for an audience. She turned to the tent and shook her head in mock dismay: 'Stop it, you show off.' A murmur of agreement went through Team Krishna. The tent, with the emotions of a two-year-old, felt hurt and misunderstood. Consequently, the sign 'Krishna Circus' lost its power, and the bulbs switched off with a pop, thereby breaking the spell and shifting the focus towards the person seated in front of the tent.

A woman with dark, hypnotic eyes and tousled hair, dressed in an oversized shirt, sat on a stool perhaps too small for her, causing her long legs to bend. Her trousers were rolled up and her feet were bare. She was doing a most unusual thing – peeling potatoes without touching them. Not sure what to do next, the Ujwala crowd stood there, gawking at Krishna. With no other option, she stared back. Thus ensued an awkward staring contest to the soundtrack of chirping birds and humans exhaling and inhaling.

Finally, the person with maximum empathy and the least amount of fear stepped forward. Atmaram Gupta spoke in an assuring whisper and extended his hand to shake Krishna's. Disoriented by the new laws of gravity and very keen to seize the opportunity, Krishna moved too quickly, stepped into the tub and was keeling over, face first, before she summoned her superpowers to break the fall without making it apparent. She fell with a gentle thud. This turn of events heralded by Krishna's apparent lack of motor coordination confused the crowd, who looked on with their heads tilted at various degrees.

Satya burst out laughing, 'Wow, that was clumsy!' Krishna's focus shifted to the man who, with his tall boots and britches, looked as if he was about to ride a horse. His laughter seemed to have no periphery and zero volume control. It was infectious, weaved its way through the filter of nervousness and fear, and emerged as an uneasy tittering from the group. Krishna caught it too – a smiling Krishna was a most heart-warming sight. So it was that the ice was finally broken.

Later, Vijendra Gupta, Mukesh Mehta, D.S. Rathore, Atmaram Gupta, Amir Hussain, Satya and Krishna sat around a tub full of wet spuds as they tried to get to the bottom of the situation. The children were too excited to sit; so they stood around pretending to be bored while stealing glances at the weird circus creatures and the magnificent tent.

Vijendra Gupta wanted to take the leading position. 'So what brings you to our little town, Ujwala?'

'Ah, that's what this place is called … Uj…wa…laaaa.' Krishna intonated each syllable with a flourish as if tutoring the residents on how to pronounce the name of their town. The children laughed at what they thought was a joke. The adults were just plain and simple offended. The combination made Krishna grumpy again. Amir Hussain decided to ask a straight question: 'So where have you come from?' 'I have come from …' Krishna said this while pointing to the sky. The conversation went downhill from there on. What ensued was less conversation and more comedy of errors. The children laughed, the adults felt ridiculed, and Krishna misunderstood. Finally, Vijendra Gupta managed to noisily push back the chair he was sitting on, even though it was set on grass: 'You know we can have you thrown off this field before you can count to three.' Krishna realised that her attempts at being conciliatory had not had the intended effect. She changed tack and spoke, looking down and into his eyes: 'Okay, then, here you go: one, two, three.' Naturally, nothing changed. So Vijendra decided to do the only thing he could to make her disappear. He turned his back and walked away. Seeing this as a decision made on behalf of all of Ujwala, everyone else followed suit. The only person standing was Satya: 'Look, I don't know who you are, but I can tell you're okay.' These first words of faith made Krishna notice his gentle eyes. 'I'm Satya, and I live close by – right there.'

'Nice to meet you, Satya.' Krishna stepped forward to shake his hand and predictably caught her foot in one of the tent's ropes. The tent was tiring of Krishna embarrassing herself, so it recoiled, moved backwards and caught her fall. There was the swishing sound of the tent's sigh of relief as it settled back to its original position. This time, Satya noticed this. Krishna caught not just the look on his face but also his hand, and shook it as vigorously as she could.

Satya felt his arm reverberating. 'And you're pretty damned strong.'

'Yes, you could say that.'

'Ummm, if I may say so, you're strong and beautiful.'

Satya wasn't entirely sure that his charm still worked, but he cocked his head and beamed anyway. Unexpectedly, Krishna looked away and half smiled.

Well, maybe I still have it, Satya thought, excited by the minor victory.

Chapter 9

The Big Show-off

Dividing and ruling was a colonial practice. A condemnable and ill-informed exercise that presumed that there could actually be two sides to anything. If one looked closely, there was only one side – the side of the good. The other side was evil and wrong. It was a good thing to have this clarity. Wheat is wheat, and chaff is chaff. It's comforting to be the wheat and not the chaff. Not having to pretend one has to 'include everyone' and the nonsense of 'equality' was liberating. There were the haves and the have-nots, he and she, human and animal, and all else in between was utter nonsense. Plus, absolutes are easier to sell. And what is life if you can't put a price on it?

Vijendra Gupta's thoughts were making their way up the stairway of his mind to perch on the high horse of being on the right side. He watched impatiently as the other members of the town huddled in the chapel once again. Nerves frayed, voices raised, and judgement clouded by anxiety because they wanted to have 'debates' and be 'democratic'. He thought about what a sham it was and how it had to be played, even if temporarily. A series of verbal jibes and undercuts later, there seemed no way to end the impasse but to put it to the dreaded 'vote': 'Okay, those in favour of letting the circus stay – put your hands up.'

When faced with the choice between what was known and what was not, the scales were tipped, and Satya was the only one left with his hand raised fully and unabashedly. There was also Rabia's meek, half-handed vote in favour of the circus staying. Goaded by this success, Vijendra Gupta wanted to drive the point home: 'Okay, those in favour of throwing the circus out – put your hands up.'

As several hands started their ascent, a loud noise interrupted them. It was an unearthly cacophony that sounded as if a brass band had hijacked the musical instruments and was now slaughtering them. As the gathering cautiously peered out of the window, they realised that their first impression was correct.

Outside the chapel, Krishna stood in a jeep she seemed to have seized from a junkyard. Surrounding her were members of her team and a rag-tag band that was ruining the reputations of the musical instruments they were bellowing through. The hands previously trying to raise themselves to vote were now clamped to protect their suffering ears.

Krishna conjured up a megaphone as if she needed a device to amplify her already thunderous voice. An ear-splitting sound emerged: 'Good evening, ladies and gentlemen, members of this lovely town. Come and watch the Krishna Circus. We promise to entertain you as you have never been entertained before. Come on. It can't hurt!'

The crowd, now curious, emerged, trying to make sense of Krishna's over-amplified and distorted words. Krishna leaned forward to nod in Satya's direction and squarely smacked herself with the megaphone. She spoke in what she thought was a whisper: 'Although *that did* hurt!' To avoid further embarrassment, Prince signalled the driver of the salvaged jeep to make a quick exit. Led by Eka, the young residents of Ujwala whooped with joy at the prospect of watching the show. And this is how a decision was arrived at that day.

The setting sun silhouetted the gilded pavilion of the Krishna Circus. The tent stopped short of pirouetting as it eagerly awaited the show that would reveal its full potential. It gladly listened to the murmuring crowd as they filed in and waited expectantly for the show to begin.

The stage shimmered, framed by deep crimson curtains, intermittently broken by paintings that seemed like vignettes from life. Forests, a river, looming mountains, blue seas and futuristic places that were unrecognizable to those in 2024. However, the themes were eternal – the vain, handsome man; the proud, wealthy woman; the couple holding hands; and the anxiety-ridden folks clutching shopping bags.

The roof of the circus consisted of layers of multicoloured fabric and well-crafted chandeliers that seemingly hung from the ceiling. A breeze that had no point of origin gently rocked the empty trapezes.

Krishna made a grand entry to the boom of rolling drums and stood atop an oversized cobalt-blue metal drum that occupied centre stage. Emphasised by a spotlight as she stood on the drum, Krishna was clearly at home: 'Ladies and gentlemen, and all the lovely children of Ujwala, welcome to Krishna Circus – a circus like no other!' The extraordinariness of the circus was not lost on the audience as they collectively leaned forward.

A tune was struck up, accompanied by the rolling of drums, forcing the audience to lean back once again into their chairs. The lighting altered, and rays of sunshine streamed in through non-existent cracks. A sweet wind parted the curtains and revealed a forest: 'Once, in a faraway forest, there lived a kind man.' With her words, a colossal tree appeared amongst the spectators. They gazed up as its autumnal leaves twirled and tittered in the wind, until it turned into a storm and blew the leaves away, revealing an army of dwarfs comfortably perched on the branches. Curiously, all the dwarfs looked like Prince.

Accompanied by the music that picked up pace, the dwarfs jumped off from great heights, which made the audience gasp. Krishna's wand safely and gently conducted them to the ground. Weaving themselves through the crowd, they made their way to centre stage: 'He loved the forest, and all its creatures were his friends.'

On cue, coloured glass bottles fell from a non-existent sky and dropped into the hands of the dwarfs, who juggled them.

The bottles increased till there were hundreds, then thousands, until finally they could no longer be counted. Always threatening to fall, the suspended bottles induced both fear and excitement. Before the former could get more prominent than the latter, the glass bottles transformed into butterflies: 'The creatures of the forest loved him like one of their own, and they lived in harmony.' Colour fluttered through the tent as butterflies flew towards the audience and flitted from shoulder to shoulder. The spectators vacillated between delight and suspicion at this incredible trickery. Before the latter could outweigh the former, Krishna recalled the butterflies with a swish of her baton.

Such magic had never been seen on Earth in 2024, and so it was that Mukesh Mehta's avaricious mind had only one thought: *How can we possess this uniqueness?* He pulled out his phone and started filming it.

Krishna's words boomed through the circus like a voice making its way through the ages: 'The seasons changed, the winter set in. Green grass gave way to a soft carpet of snow. With it came scarcity of food, but everyone in the forest knew how to share, and they continued in harmony.' Now there was deep winter in the circus. Flakes of snow fell upon shoulders without touching them. They left no trace on the ground; they flitted like thoughts and disappeared.

Anita and an identical band of cyclists entered the fray. Their pristine white bodies were almost invisible against the white falling snow. They turned, circled and jumped, all while forming apparitions of animals in the forest. Sometimes they were lions with manes, and at other times they were foxes and squirrels. If the audience had a collective jaw, it would have dropped to the floor. Krishna decided that this was the moment to take it up a notch, so she raised her baton, and the cyclists floated up like they were notes suspended by the soaring music. As they levitated with their bicycles, they amalgamated and formed a large creature – possibly a man, maybe an ogre. He was dressed in a long, pin-striped coat, matching pants and shiny shoes that seemed too large for his feet, and carried a peculiar basket that could be mistaken for a briefcase. 'Until … until Mr Banks started to snatch and store all kinds of riches from the forest.' The giant apparition that seemed to grow with every passing minute made his way on to the stage with a series of thuds. The music, now a large howl, conjured up a pack of hyenas that tailed the apparition. They hissed and spat as they echoed his every move. With his mouth open, Mr Banks drew, like a magnet, all the resources of the forest and devoured them hungrily. 'He took the food, he took the shelter, and he took the creatures and made them work in the cold, cold winter.'

On dark horses and dressed like warriors rode Maya, accompanied by several other Mayas. They held the reins tight even as the horses neighed and bucked, making a declaration of war. Ryan answered this battle cry. He made an entry with his battalion that looked like rogue elephants, and atop each of these animals was Ryan and his many duplicates. They stomped and trumpeted, readying for a fight. 'So it is that they now scrambled for the scarce resources. In stepped Mr Banks, who loaned them fears and more reasons to hate. The forest was no longer peaceful, but a battleground, and a large, dark cloud loomed over the woods.'

Ryan's and Maya's armies clashed, and the circus was shrouded in fog. It grew thick enough to obscure audience members, and the people of Ujwala felt isolated and alone. It did not help that sighs of desolation and cries of despair filled their ears. 'But … but … but … then … the kind man started to beat the drum of the forest that struck when there was a catastrophe. It silenced those who fought, and drew all the creatures with its call. They gathered in a circle as they were accustomed to.'

A slow drumbeat echoed through the circus. With each stroke, the clouds cleared to reveal Krishna standing on the drum, now transformed into a man with a baritone. 'Forest dwellers, we are one. Our bodies may seem different, our colours are varied, and we like to eat different things, but underneath, we are all the same. We are the forest, and the forest is us. We are made of nature, and nature of us. We must love and not hate; unite, not divide; and live as one – it is the only true way to thrive and survive.' With each of Krishna's words, the circus transformed once more and became not a place for battle but celebration.

The music raised its tempo and Krishna returned to her original form. 'His words brought back the memory of the time when they lived in peace and harmony, and there was enough for all. A decision was taken to end the reign of Mr Banks. They schemed and laid a trap, and Mr Banks fell right in.'

Mr Banks, the plunderer, was heaving in an attempt to rise from the crevice he had fallen into. With his efforts he moved the entire circus threatening to topple it. The tent rocked like a boat in a storm, adults quivered in fear, and the children of Ujwala squealed with joy. Then the creatures on stage did a strange thing – they embraced and comforted Mr Banks as if he were a baby. And with that, the circus stabilised again: 'The creatures of the forest brought him out, and instead of hurting him, they gave him love and compassion and many beautiful berries.' In the circus, the forest was at the peak of spring. Flowers bloomed, and their scent floated towards the audience. 'They left him outside the forest to spread the kindness that he had received. And once more, the forest was full of joy, sunshine and abundance.'

The tent's penultimate moment was filled with blooming flowers, bees, birds and butterflies. They moved like instruments, playing the same notes in unison, becoming a symphony of colour. As the music peaked, a golden light flooded the tent. Finally, the music gradually faded to silence. The audience sat transfixed with unblinking eyes, elated and moved. They felt both fulfilled and still wanted more. Then the curtain fell, and the residents of Ujwala broke into thunderous applause.

Typically, it was Jeet and Eka who found their voices first.

Jeet saw a plot. 'This is not normal – there's something weird happening here, no?'

Eka was less cynical. 'No, I believe it. Yes, I have faith that there is nothing that weird going on here!'

Satya had forgotten to clap. He sat with his hands by his side even as the audience's ovations continued. He knew there was nothing usual about the performance, but he did not care: *If this is magic, it's the best kind there is!* The euphoria of the audience spelt worry for Mukesh Mehta. Getting the circus off this field would now be a bigger challenge.

Outside the tent, a full moon made the grass sparkle, and the river looked like a stream of silver, but no one paid them any heed, their voices reduced to whispers in reverence for what they had witnessed. They were awestruck as they left the Krishna Circus. Even Vijendra Gupta felt compelled to exclaim, 'Fantastic! I would love to see it again.' Elation and joy accompanied them as they made their way home. Such is the power of art that a community at odds minutes ago now felt integrated by an inspiring vision. Art will always have that place – the universal connector. The opposite of the divider and ruler.

Chapter 10

All That Glitters

Gold is gold, silver is silver, money is money, and somebody has to have it. What is the use of bounty if it cannot be possessed? Absolutely nothing. And if you have it, flaunt it. Otherwise, what is the use of possessing it? Absolutely none.

There is no end to human imagination, but in some instances, its curtailment is not a bad idea. To halt it right before it runs amok and causes its absurd mental machinations to bear on the world at large. A living example of this was the building that housed Wholly Treat Foods Inc. It was a mass of tortured, twisted metal, interspersed with glass. These glass sheets doubled up as screens. In what space was left, the walls had smatterings of canvases that were unlikely to qualify as art. The net product was a distorted, crushed blob with shrieking images that told tales of great profitability. Visually, it was an all-loss, zero-profit proposition. The people who worked here wore serious expressions and dark suits. They walked up and down with a declared purpose to never be viewed as expendable. The endeavour was to look like products of the same factory.

Breaking this picture of control and consistency came a ticking Mukesh Mehta. MM – the miracle man who still functioned, even though he felt like he might have swallowed a clock. It got a thorough winding up as he made his way to the big boss's office, carrying in his throat words that the chief would not like to hear. But no one dared look at him strangely because he was, after all, the second in command.

Mukesh Mehta disembarked from the lift and straightened his tie. Number 1 and Number 2 – the chief's henchmen intercepted him and took him on a long walk down the corridor, as if on a pilgrimage, where the duration of the walk was in direct proportion to the importance of the entity at the end of it.

MM slowed down in a bid to postpone the inevitable. In addition to his other afflictions, he now broke into a sweat. After all, it was none other than Mr Tamas Lobha. *The* Tamas Lobha, the all-powerful and the richest and owner/master of Wholly Treat Foods. He could do anything and get away with it. This man had everyone in his tweeny-weeny pocket. Yes, his magic pocket that, despite its size, had accommodated many monsters and his ego that was taller and bigger than any earthly creature.

Number 1 and Number 2 sensed MM's hesitation. They stepped forward, opened the oversized door and practically pushed him through it – the prey was in the cage.

Behind a large ornate desk, almost eclipsed by it, sat a small man with large hands. They were placed on the table that reflected every shape and colour of the various gems embedded in the rings on his fingers. These stones were supposed to provide him with astrological protection but were also large enough to work as knuckledusters. His shock of grey hair reflected the white light in the office and made it look as if he was wearing a steel plate on his head. On the upside, it coordinated fashionably with his yellow-and-grey pin-striped suit with collars so broad that they ran right off his shoulders.

But the most noteworthy feature was Lobha's face. His prominent bulbous nose and the deep scar that split his face in half told you the other side of the story that the trappings did not. The story of how he had managed to rise from the ranks and reach the dizzying heights of dirty money. As he looked over his nose at his second-in-command–cum–punching bag, he gauged from his physical unease that he came bearing bad news. Lobha looked at his rather large and expensive watch and thought about the time he was about to waste and how he could make it interesting. MM recognised the signal that his boss was preparing to ignore him for the next ten minutes.

Predictably, Lobha turned his back on MM and towards his rather large television to watch a particularly bloody boxing match. The blood flew without restraint, and Lobha did not flinch. Eventually, he stifled a yawn and spoke disinterestedly: 'You've got to love blood.' The men who worked in his office looked up briefly from their small desks to violently agree with him. The five women in short skirts pretended their aural capacities had deserted them and carried on with the activity of serving beverages even as a man was beaten to death on screen.

Lobha turned off the TV and turned to MM – from one source of entertainment to another – from the high of violence to the exhilaration of power: 'Welcome, Mukesh. Have you come here to display your utter inability to do anything properly?' Lobha was leaning back in his chair, watching his minion squirm and enjoying it. In the silence that followed the rhetorical question, MM found the strength to speak – 'Sir, sir, sir … it, it's … entirely … completely, absolutely … depends … how, how … you see the circus … is a a marvel…'

Lobha sensed that Mukesh Mehta's trip was not a complete washout, and he leaned forward. MM took the cue to play back video recordings of the circus performance. Everyone watched, riveted and intrigued. Tamas Lobha knew there was an opportunity there. 'How are they doing this stuff?' All the shoulders in the room shrugged, and no mouth moved to hazard any guess. Tamas Lobha raised his eyebrows as the mind behind his creased forehead turned and made some quick calculations. Then, there on the screen, enlarged and grainy but still larger than life, stood Krishna, her wild mane, her body arched as she raised her wand, and her mouth turned upwards between a smile and a laugh. She was clearly at home. Lobha's forehead was now uncrumpled, and his eyes narrowed as he fixed his gaze: 'The ringmaster is a *woman*?' And that's how Mukesh

Mehta's twitch subsided, and a smile rose to his lips. It transformed his face enough for him to look like his happier cousin: 'Exactly my point, sir. That show was extraordinary, and of course, people just took to it, and they want the circus to stay.'

'Yes, but we want it off the meadow.'

'Sir, may I suggest, sir … As you well know … there is nothing that money can't buy. So we … we start by paying her some money and sponsoring the circus.'

Tamas Lobha listened with his ears pricked as MM had his first good idea.

'Our name goes up over the circus, sir … and then, sir, she will move on, and we stay, sir!'

Tamas Lobha's response was a loud, reassuring laugh. 'That's a good plan. But I want to get my hands on the technology as well.' Mukesh Mehta nodded too vigorously leading to a short spell of dizziness. Lobha jumped off his chair, walked around the table, and stepped on a small stool. Now he was almost at MM's height. He spoke in a raspy whisper, as if MM were a priest and he the confessor: 'Why don't you bring her here for a meeting?'

While simultaneously coping with nodding-induced vertigo and still continuing the head bobbing, MM was thinking, *Easier said than done.*

As MM made his way out of Lobha's lair, he thought about what a shitty few days it had been, and felt sorry for himself.

Chapter 11

Revelations

Is it possible to have a being that is not an animal as your friend and compatriot? To both love and be loved by it? Or is it just affection one conjures up because you have spent the whole of your lives together? Either way, knowing that this one relationship would not change makes it comforting.

Krishna's thoughts floated languidly like paper boats on placid waters as she marvelled at the circus tent she had come to love so much. Today, it had a sunny yellow hue as it stood swaying in the wind, its awnings gently rocking and the flags waving in the breeze. Still, Krishna felt mired by the lack of information. It had been such a long journey, and she was ready to fulfil the prophecy, but clueless about the hows and the whys. She stared at the tent, hoping an answer would magically reveal itself. Instead, in one of its many mood swings, the tent shuddered and consequently popped a few blue bulbs on the sign, making it read 'KR SHNA CIRC S'.

Lost in her contemplation and unmindful of who might be watching, Krishna soared to the top and stood mid-air, fixing the busted bulbs. She paused for a moment to see if there was something she had missed. All she saw was the green meadow, a silver-blue river with white cackling rapids, and a small town with winding roads. Krishna sighed, made her way back to the ground, and found Satya blocking her way like he was the last bastion standing between Ujwala and disaster: 'So, what's the plan? I hear you're going to sell out to them. Let Wholly Treat Foods take over?'

Although taken aback, Krishna understood Satya's confusion and answered as she always did, with complete honesty: 'Oh, god knows! Truth be told, I'm not even in charge of myself enough to sell out. I am sent to unknown places, on unknown missions, and I leave when the work is done. I cannot control my arrival or departure – it's a bit annoying, but that's exactly how it is.' She wanted to tell him everything from the start, but he wasn't asking the right questions or in the correct order. As now he wanted to know: 'So who is your boss?' Krishna sighed and replied even as she realised it would only baffle him further: 'This tent. It decides where we go and when we leave. I have to discover my mission and complete it.'

Satya seemed to be contemplating what to say next. He seemed to be struggling, and then, much to her relief, he asked the right questions: 'Who are you, Krishna? Where are you from?'

Krishna rolled the question around in her mind and wondered if she could trust him. 'If I tell you, will you believe me?' Krishna held her hand out to look for confirmation of his commitment. To her surprise, Satya took her extended hand and gently placed it on his arm. 'Come, let's take a little walk, and you can tell me your story.'

The wind whistled, the river gushed, the birds twittered, the crickets croaked, and their feet rustled through the grass. To this symphony of nature, Krishna drew the curtain back and revealed her life so far. 'I was born in Kams's realm – Mathura. He is the king of Mathura.'

Satya's eyes darted with confusion. 'Oh … Kams? Mathura? King?'

'If any of this is too confusing, please feel free to stop me,' she said.

Satya answered almost too soon: 'No, no, it's not confusing at all. Go on, please.'

Krishna looked at Satya to check if he was indeed telling the truth. She wasn't sure, but he did look curious enough for her to continue. 'It is Mathura that exists in the future, a hundred years from now. Capiche?' Satya wanted to believe Krishna. Still, first, he needed to transcend his lifetime of not casually meeting time travellers. He decided it might be best to reconfirm what he was hearing. 'Ah, a hundred years from now?'

Krishna nodded and continued, 'So … no child was born in Mathura because of an augury.' Satya repeated after her, but only with question marks: 'An augury? No children?'

Krishna stopped and looked Satya straight in the eye: 'Are you going to repeat everything I say?'

Satya had to smile at Krishna's exasperation. He walked away and beckoned Krishna to follow him to the river that sparkled and ran in a great hurry towards its destination. Krishna touched its surface and marvelled at its extraordinariness; nature was the only real artist she knew – always original, relevant and capable of creating that which cannot be humanly conceived. Satya leaned back and seemed to be ready to hear what she had to say. 'Please go on. I promise not to interrupt.'

The duo sat dangling their feet in the shimmering, cool water as she talked about her birth, Parshuram, her biological parents, Devaki and Vasu, and her most beloved mother – Yashoda.

Satya had heard the names of these characters so very often – it was part of the mythology he grew up with. Now hearing another version of it, it dawned upon him with rising panic that sitting near him was not just 'The Saviour', but if her story was true, Krishna perhaps was an avatar of the creator. Yet he had to accept every word she said or nothing at all. He searched Krishna's earnest face and was relieved by the decision that came to him – he now settled in and braced himself to go with the flow. The sun moved closer to the horizon as Krishna went on with her story.

'I was a few hours old when my adoptive mother Yashoda leapt into the portal with me. She looked after me, protected me and taught me everything I know. It was perilous because the residents of Kams's Mathura have trackers implanted in their bodies. Kams didn't have access to the portal, but it was possible that Parshuram might crack under pressure. So we travelled from one time dimension to another, always training, learning and becoming stronger.'

Satya imagined little Krishna preparing to become a warrior with the weight of saving the world on her little shoulders, and his heart went out to her.

'We did not have a house or a permanent abode; so I learnt to make my home where my mother was. She was my teacher, parent, sibling and friend.' The evening breeze turned to a stronger wind; so Satya took off his jacket and put it on Krishna's shoulders. The ordinariness of the gesture touched Krishna, and she leaned in to rest her head on Satya's chest. There was comfort in his even, unchanging heartbeat.

Krishna described the training, which included martial arts, breathing exercises, endurance and strength training and meditation. Her words made it all come alive for Satya. He saw Krishna growing up without a carefree childhood, where she spent every moment in preparation for what was her destiny – to save the world. And yet, she was neither troubled by it nor did she long for anything else. Krishna could be strong and weak, intelligent and silly, worldly-wise and naive. She managed to sail down the river with her feet in two different boats – perfectly balanced in a world of opposites. He wondered how that came to be. As if reading his mind, she answered, 'My mother Yashoda taught me that mind control was the key to everything. The access and control of my powers lay in the control of my mind.'

'How can one control one's mind?'

'She taught me an ancient meditation practice called Kriya Yoga. On the surface, it's just a breathing technique, but when it's taught and practised properly, it has the power to help control one's mind.'

'Wish I could learn that! Could you teach it to me?'

'Well, it is ancient enough to be present even now on Earth. We need to find the right teacher – someone who will continue on this earth plane while you are here. You understand?'

Satya understood the import of Krishna's words, and it made him sad to recognise the impermanence of her presence. He thought a tear was making its way out of his eye. He blinked it away and decided to make the most of their time together. Krishna lifted her head to look at him. He did want to look her in the eye but his courage failed him, and he spoke as he scanned the darkening horizon: 'Please continue.'

'You see, in the future, a hundred years from now, the Jamakhors, who are people afflicted with extreme greed: raided and plundered the Earth until they diminished or, in this case, will diminish all earthly resources, leaving our planet devoid of any nature or life. The Jamakhors are here now, but as time goes on, they will become all-powerful and have no opposition.'

Satya was positively riveted but wondered how Krishna would halt the march of the greedy: 'And you?'

'I must travel back in time to all those instances when the destruction of Earth was seeded, and reverse it, thus, changing the course of history and restoring Earth and its dignity to its creatures. I am the "avatar" that will save the Earth.' Krishna said the last sentence softly and confirmed Satya's belief. Her words lacked any hint of hyperbole; he looked at Krishna with fresh eyes. She seemed to have emerged from the golden beam of the setting sun that framed her. 'I am here to save the earth and finish Kams – the last and most powerful of the Jamakhors. He will diminish as I undo each turn in history that leads to our planet's destruction. Kams will lose his power, and his world will slowly disintegrate.'

While admiring her calm even as she talked about ending the most powerful man, Satya felt immobilised by the magnitude of her mission, and he feared that he had turned to stone as he struggled to react. Krishna seemed not to notice the effect of her words on him and smiled – her teeth unabashedly exposed, her eyes crinkling with mirth. Then she spoke amidst emerging laughter: 'And you know all avatars have a weapon, right?'

Krishna extended her hand towards the ground and opened her palm. Expecting something dangerous to appear, Satya leapt up in fright. Ultimately, it was an overreaction because Krishna conjured up a delicate silver baton that looked more like a flute. 'And this is my weapon. With it, I can conduct life like an orchestra – see ...' She flourished her weapon and made small rocks move. With a turn of her wrist, she changed them into little colourful birds. 'This is my favourite part – the transformations.'

'It is pretty impressive!'

Satya should not have felt fear, but he was inadvertently inching away. Krishna asked him to sit down as she put away the baton, thus restoring the rocks to their original state. 'Oh, what does it matter – it is just matter. A rose by any other name is still a rose or not a rose – it is all the same, really.'

Satya had never heard the metaphor used quite this way and did not know what she was alluding to. Well, he thought – in for a penny, in for a pound.

'Go on, please.'

'Then, as I found my feet and learnt everything I needed to know, it was time for my mother to leave. She feared her tracker would be a liability. She left me, but not without the promise that she would return. I remember her words clearly: "Child, now you know how time and space work, and so you know that no one ever goes away. Time is just a curtain that we may part if we want to. I will always be there."'

The sun was making its way below the horizon, but not without highlighting the river's frothy waves with its crimson rays. Krishna and Satya listened to its babble that sounded like complaints about the sun's waning attention. 'She told me that the tent would be my guide to all the time and events for missions, and that I must trust it. The tent also helped me find my compatriots – my team and my new family.'

With the sun's departure, the stars came out, one billion at a time, and the moon took its place amongst them, further illuminating the darkness.

'I found Anita in the year 2091. There was a chemical leak. She survived but had lost skin pigmentation. Anita, the androgynous beauty, had mutated, and with it, she gained the power to regenerate and become one with plant life.'

'And Prince?'

'Ah, Prince! I found him in 1956, in the depths of the earth, below a circus. The world is a cruel place for those who are different; especially the ones perceived as weak. He has a deep relationship with the soul of the earth. Prince has the power to burrow into its depths. He was in a deep hole when I found him, if you know what I mean?' Krishna laughed at full throttle; a guffaw that echoed through the mountains that now glistened under the moon's rays.

'Ryan is the strongest man you've ever met. In 1425, he was a local attraction. He could pull and move any object – carts, horses and even elephants. They didn't know that he was downplaying his strength for fear of scaring those around him. Ryan suspected he did not belong in the world of the 'normals', as he liked to call the rest of humanity, and when he met me, he knew he was right.'

Satya thought about Team Krishna. They seemed odd, but were instead extraordinary. He wondered if there were more like them – these people who can transcend the ordinariness that binds humans to the mundane confines of life on Earth.

'It was the year 2002; Maya was drugged and imprisoned in a science laboratory. She can read minds. The only condition is the presence of fear. If you have fear within you, Maya can play with your mind and rearrange your thoughts. In 2002, Earth was replete with fear, when people found out that Maya had become a threat. We did not exchange words; Maya understood who I was and where she was going.' Krishna smiled to herself, and Satya could feel her joy at having found her co-travellers. 'And, about the tent – I'm here now, and we will find out if the tent was right to bring me here.'

At a not-so-appropriate moment, Satya's scepticism returned with a misplaced sense of humour: 'One can only hope, because right now it seems as if you travelled a very long way to save one little meadow and a small town. It's hardly the mission for a superhero meant to save the world, right?'

But Krishna hardly noticed what he was saying as she returned to her contemplations. 'There's got to be more … the tent can't be wrong…'

So, Satya persevered, 'Or maybe this is all a sinister plan to finish the world, one potato chip at a time?' Satya's nervous humour wasn't landing as well as he had intended. Krishna did not laugh but looked away, frowning into the landscape. Satya was grappling for a way to end the conversation impasse when the awkward silence was broken by the sound of helicopters making their way through the night sky of Ujwala.

'Damn these choppers! They've been going over the village too often for the last six months. They are extremely noisy and manage to disturb both the peace and my bees.'

Krishna' felt her instinct nudging her to walk towards the middle of the field. It was here that the helicopters seemed to circle. She wondered why it was *this*, an empty meadow, that they chose to survey consistently. Satya followed her to the spot in time to see her expression transform from puzzled to relieved. Right before his eyes, Krishna squared her shoulders and stood to full height, and with a wave of her baton, she was in a blue bodysuit and a headdress crowned with peacock feathers. It was clear from the way she inhabited the costume that this was where she belonged. And then, just like that, without bluff or bluster,

Krishna lifted a knee and flew up into the darkness. Satya had seen this so many times in superhero films, but in real life, it was not as reassuring – it scared him and made him want to run. Yet, he stood rooted to the spot, unable to take his eyes off her as she made her way across the sky.

Krishna realised that there were more choppers than usual – six in all. If it was what she suspected, she would have to fly below the moving helicopters to confirm. What she was looking for was right there – a machine for the magnetic mapping of the earth. She hovered to take a closer look and learn more about the device. Krishna failed to notice one of the pilots who looked like he was struggling with the dilemma of seeing a woman flying in the sky and believing it.

The pilot looked out of his window as he always did. He saw a woman in a blue bodysuit, perpendicular to the helicopter, peering at the bottom of the chopper. He did think about reporting it, but then blamed it on his new stash of fine Malana. So instead, he panicked quietly and called the reconnaissance mission off. They did an about-turn, and Krishna made her way back down to the field. She put her ear to the ground and got a sign, but she needed to get it confirmed.

Satya was trying to contain his utter shock by feigning casualness: 'Hey, so how was it up there?'

Krishna ran, her feet now accustomed to Earth's gravitational pull. She made her way to the circus in no time, leaving Satya – who hadn't had a chance to catch his breath – behind. Hearing the commotion, Anita and Prince stepped out of the tent. Krishna practically hauled Prince to the centre of the field. 'Please dig deep. I think our mission is here, under the soil.' The instruction exhilarated Prince. It would be the first time he would put his superpower to its actual use. 'The question is, how deep?' Prince barrelled into the earth like a diver in the sea. He cut through it like it was merely air. Soon, he was no longer visible.

Satya's conception of reality had been seriously challenged lately. Now Prince's display of his superpowers defeated him, and he sat down – resigned. Anita sympathetically patting him on the shoulder did not improve his state of mind.

Krishna peered down into the depths where Prince seemed to have stopped. 'Did you find anything?'

Prince's voice carried up and confirmed what Krishna suspected: 'There are shining … rocks that look as if they are made of silver. It looks like uranium. This is uranium.' Krishna knew this wasn't good, but she felt a sense of relief in any case. 'And that's why the river glistens!' she exclaimed.

Prince emerged, leaving a ditch in his wake. Anita stepped in and restored the earth and its plant life. There was no way of telling that, minutes ago, there was a gaping hole in its place.

Satya felt like he was in a foreign movie with no subtitles; he watched but couldn't keep up. 'What? I wish someone would tell me what's going on.' Someone needed to attend to Satya. He was in a circle of superheroes and wanted to talk about it. He wanted to be heard: 'It's hard enough to see someone flying around and people you know … doing the things you do…'

Krishna knew there would be time to attend to Satya's confusion, but right now, it seemed like her mission, *the* mission, needed her unwavering concentration. It was comforting to know that her superhero family was around her. 'Here is where the mining will start, but to what end?' Krishna said this as she looked to Maya to answer the question.

Maya was already scanning minds and finding the future, and what it would hold. 'They're not just mining but also going to build nuclear weapons, leading to an … apocalypse. Annihilation.'

Krishna let the import of the words sink in. This was it. Her first mission was at hand. It seemed simple enough. Perhaps it was chosen to ease her in. But she couldn't help but think back to Yashoda's words: 'I pray that you come away unharmed from your first mission.' She wondered if there was more that was to play out. She reached out to her team and they all stood holding hands, realising that their mission had begun.

Satya wanted to believe that the group in front of him was crazy – that would be the sanest explanation for the situation. But he also knew that this wasn't the case. The team had shown themselves to be robust, dependable and mostly affable. Satya gaped in surprise as Krishna exclaimed, 'So you see? The tent is never wrong. I was worried for a bit there.'

'Oh, you were worried then, and now you're not?' Satya's tone tempted Maya. He was fear-ridden, and his brain was rife for her to enter. What she saw made her look at Satya anew. She saw a child, alone in a large home with a silent mother and an unavailable patriarch for a father. The communication was adequate but not quite enough to include understanding. Maya was privy to his struggle to conform and yet the longing to escape the shackles of the mundane as his only unswerving life motives. Maya's eyes softened as she realised that Satya – brave enough to go against all societal expectations – was full of fear and confusion, faced now with Krishna, her team and their superpowers. Satya suspected Maya was probing him. *Is she in my mind?* he thought and, without realising, started walking away in a hurry. He had no idea how that turned into a sprint until it dawned upon him that he was running away from Krishna and company.

Krishna was new to the world of missions and human beings. Especially one like Satya – he invoked a feeling within her that she was not used to: 'He seems so strange.'

'Compared to us, you mean?' Maya was holding back her laughter. There was a moment of recognition as they saw themselves through Satya's eyes. Ryan was the first to laugh, and everyone followed suit. Maya caught the look in Krishna's eyes. Even as she laughed, her eyes were trained in a particular direction.

Krishna caught up with Satya as he sat on his front porch, staring at the sparkling night sky. Krishna stepped forward tentatively so as to not startle him. Surprisingly, Satya seemed relieved to see her: 'I'm glad you came, and I'm sorry I … you know it was all a bit too much to handle.'

'Oh yes. I should have known that, and I'm sorry about that too.'

She sat beside him and looked out into the night. Moments passed as they sat in silence. Then Krishna slipped her hand into his. Satya, in turn, lifted their clasped hands and kissed hers. 'Krishna, I don't think we can … it's a bit hard knowing that your partner is a superhero. Also, I don't think long-distance would work for us.'

Krishna wanted to think this was possible. 'I see your point, but couldn't we just live in the moment? Be together while we are?'

'No. I'm only human after all.'

Krishna smiled at Satya's repeated attempts at humour in a bid to lighten a moment that was difficult for him.

'I agree with you.' Krishna said this in the most conciliatory way, but she thought Satya looked disappointed as he said, 'Well, thank you.'

'Satya, I have a favour to ask. You must come with me to meet the big boss of Whole whatever foods.'

Satya knew he had a chance, and he took it. 'Okay, I'll go with you.'

Krishna's face lit up, and this, in turn, made Satya smile.

Chapter 12

A Deal Is Struck

Everything looks different when you haven't slept. They say sleep makes you live longer and live younger. Well, I feel as if I am a hundred years old today. And this stuffy windowless office isn't helping.

Satya stifled a yawn and blamed it on the revelations of the night before. His nightmares included being sucked into black holes, lifted by a flying Krishna, and being dropped to the ground with force. Now he was not exactly sure why he had agreed to come, fighting sleep, foreboding and irritability. It did not help that Mukesh Mehta spoke with a voice similar to chalk on a board: 'Please behold what is is is … who is is inside. Please and please behold …' Before MM could extend his eulogy any further, one of the strongmen pushed the door open, revealing what looked like an ornate desk with no one behind it – until Tamas Lobha shifted and craned his head.

At first sight, he looked like a pleasant man with a good temper. Then he propelled himself out of the chair and made his way over to Krishna, extending a hand as if doing her a favour. Lobha reminded her of a nineteenth-century thug rather than the head of a world-class corporation. Krishna's befuddlements led to her inadvertently failing to secure Lobha's hand. Satya stepped in and took it, hoping to halt Lobha's self-worth from plummeting. It did not help, and Lobha retreated to his throne-like chair and put his large desk between himself and the duo that faced him. Krishna and Satya sank into the over-upholstered chairs that felt like buckets of quicksand. They clung on to the ornate arms of the chair in a bid to avoid being sucked in.

Krishna scanned the room. On a velvety, red, soft board, pinned with white drawing pins, was a testament to how human beings always take something good and turn it into a fatal consequence for humanity. There were enlarged black-and-white images of Hiroshima, Fukushima, Chernobyl, The Three Mile nuclear disaster, and others.

On the other side of the room was a map of the world. It was backlit and mounted on glass. Bright yellow light streamed through and cast shadows, making lucid impressions of land masses on those around. There was China on a few cheeks, Canada on an arm, Italy rippling on a shirt and Madagascar on a skirt that flitted as it moved.

Lobha chose this moment to address Krishna: 'Welcome to the biggest corporation in India and maybe the world. Should we get straight to business?' The most notable feature on the map was Ujwala. It burned brighter than the others, with specific locations pinpointed. Having Krishna's eyes on his plan slightly dented Lobha's hubris. He signalled to his minions and, instantly, the world was plunged into darkness.

Krishna turned to Lobha and conjured up a counterfeit smile through gritted teeth as she spoke. 'So what can I do for you?'

Krishna had expected Lobha to speak, but instead, it was his marionette MM. 'Well, well, you see, we are … offering, you know … that thing is …' Krishna wondered when he would get to the point until she saw Tamas Lobha do what she never expected him to – he rolled his eyes and raised his hand to get MM to cease his chatter. Then he spoke while looking Krishna straight in the eye: 'We would like to buy your circus. Naturally, there are a few conditions.' Lobha indicated to Mukesh Mehta to come alive again. The communication was like one from a ventriloquist to his dummy. MM pushed forward what looked like a novella but was, in fact, a contract. 'We agree … to money … but you agree … must to terminologies and terms …'

Satya, who had been hoping that Lobha's plush office might have a pantry that could produce strong black coffee, was disappointed because no one even brought it up. It pushed his irritation to anger. He channelled some of it as he glowered at MM and prepared to tell him what was on his mind until Krishna jumped in. 'Fine. Agreed. Make the payment in his name.' She said this while pointing in Satya's direction.

MM seemed shocked by this turn of events. 'Don't you read it? Want to?'

Krishna answered swiftly and honestly, 'No.'

The play had moved off-script, and a dead silence ensued. Krishna jumped into the silence and signed the contract in what seemed like a whirl because it was indeed just that. Satya brought out his wallet made from recycled fabric and retrieved a neat note with his bank account details written with a fountain pen and handed it to MM, and spoke through gritted teeth: 'Also, can I get a really strong black coffee? With four spoons of sugar?'

MM looked like he might catch the Coronavirus from the piece of paper, and held it by its corners while scratching his face. Lobha indicated to one of the thus-far invisible women, and Satya watched in gratitude as she made her way to the pantry. Mukesh Mehta pored over the signed novella, aka contract, and noticed that it had indeed been signed.

Moments later, Satya hyper-palpitated as he ingested the surprisingly good coffee while Krishna tried to make small talk and failed. Then the sound of a bird from Satya's phone announced the arrival of the promised amount in his bank account. This brought the meeting to an end. Krishna sprang up with more eagerness than was called for, and finally took Lobha's hand and shook it till he vibrated like jelly on a revving car bonnet.

Following this, Krishna and Satya left. Lobha and Mehta stared in the direction of their exit longer than they should have. They got what they wanted; so why didn't it feel right? But there was no one there who would call out the lack of the emperor's attire; so everyone pretended all was well.

Outside, in the long corridor, Satya and Krishna smiled at each other. It was their Bonnie and Clyde moment; but Krishna did not know it yet. They held hands as they exited the glass monument of greed, feeling richer in more ways than one.

Chapter 13

The Field

Here I am. Sturdy. Strong. Resilient. Pliable. Pretty. Pleasing. And my existence is in service of human beings. I breathe in their polluted air and breathe out life for them. I give them the vital thing that they need to stay alive. And they stamp all over me and cover me with trash. Sigh! They're just being human, I guess.

The grass on the vast field wasn't feeling as enthusiastic as the crowds that came, ate and trailed their trash like Hansel and Gretel over its surface. Then there were the full bladders being emptied with abandon. Let's face it – a clean environment isn't for everyone.

For all the calculations, Wholly Treat Foods Inc did not expect this turnout, and they were thrilled. With the teeming audience came another circus with their vans, flashing bulbs and reporters who flooded multiple microphones with assumptions.

Satya found Krishna staring at the pandemonium with perfect detachment. They stood away from the fracas, but it was, clearly, not far enough. A car came to a screeching halt, almost brushing Satya's dusty boots. This disregard for personal space was typical of his ilk – Nikhil Mandal was a journalist. His lanky frame and serious face had travelled far and wide in search of stories to break. He came to Ujwala drawn by descriptions of the circus performance. Nikhil had been around long enough to know there was more to it than met the eye.

From where Satya and Krishna stood, they saw him as the man in a green kurta, a beige waistcoat and large eyes behind oversized spectacles that scanned the horizon like a sniper. His eyes finally rested on Satya. As he spoke, he enunciated each word as if speaking to a child: 'I'm a reporter from the *National Times*. I want to write about this otherworldly circus everyone is talking about. Do you know where I can find the person who runs this circus – Krishna?'

Satya raised his thumb and pointed in Krishna's direction, as if he were hitching a ride out of Nikhil's view. Nikhil turned his gaze and was intrigued. She was neither demure, smiling to please, petite or terribly symmetrical, yet she was so attractive. Nikhil had a world view where beauty and brains did not reside on the same premises. Consequently, Nikhil smiled, lowered his voice and spoke to Krishna slowly: 'Hi. I want to meet someone who can tell me about the circus. Can you take me to Krishna, please?'

Amongst the din, Anita emerged in her cycling costume looking like a resplendent, unbaked porcelain statue – devoid of any pigmentation and as elegant. Anita beckoned Krishna, and they walked away against the backdrop of a gobsmacked Nikhil. If Krishna found his expression amusing, she did not betray it and spoke in an even tone: 'Best you watch the show first.'

At the other end of town, Atmaram was catching up with his friends. They were doing some time travelling by behaving like their former selves from half a century ago.

Atmaram played a song from the days of yore and yielded to the sentimentality of the lyrics, swaying his head, his hands involuntarily tapping an old chinar wood table and smiling as the floodgates of memory opened. The tune seemed to have no effect on Rathore and Hussain, who were locked in fierce competition as they took their places on either side of a chessboard. It was clear the pieces on the board were no longer just a mock formation of a confrontation.

Devendra Singh Rathore stroked his handlebar moustache as he urged Hussain, 'You take too damn long to make a move. I don't have the patience for your indecisiveness. If you were in a war, you would have gone to heaven by now.' Hussain, on the other hand, had dug his heels in as he prepared to win and answered, 'That's why you always lose. War is tactical. One needs brains, not just muscles – understood, mister?' An argument with raised voices ensued as Atmaram accused them of disturbing his peace. 'I'm going home. You people are so loud. You have zero … *andaa* appreciation for the arts. Bloody philistines!' Amir Hussain felt particularly hurt as he considered himself the aesthete of the group. 'We are philistines but you are the one who listens to soppy sentimental Bollywood music? Wah bhai, wah!'

Atmaram had run out of words to insult them, and he chose instead to stick his tongue out. Then he picked up his walking stick and, in the process, tipped over a silver vase. The metal struck the marble floor loud enough for its echo to carry to the town square, where large trucks and bulldozers positioned themselves silhouetted against the moonlight. Rathore raised his voice to an army order decibel: 'Why did you drop the vase? Why? Are you crazy? Or are you senile?'

Atmaram Gupta's last pedantic act had triggered his friends, arguing heatedly while the singer on the soundtrack had become a plaintiff for love, pleading at the highest musical note available to him. This combination of crescendos obscured the sounds of machines and people getting ready to destroy their beloved Ujwala. Before Atmaram could respond with his sharpest retort, he was halted by a shattering sound that made the fall of the vase sound like a tinkling call bell. They rushed to the source of the crash just in time to see a bulldozer crashing through a building.

While on one end of the town these old friends realised that a plan was at play, on the other end, on the field, it coincided with the end of Krishna's performance – the monkey took it all. He lived happily in the warm sun while the cats sat empty-handed in the pouring rain. Nikhil Mandal sat in the tent where it was raining, but no one got wet. The sun was shining, but no one was hot. He had expected good, even excellent, but this was more than that. The thundering applause continued. Shockingly, no one questioned how it came to be. Nikhil blamed people's unquestioning submission, believing everything they see, for all the ills in the world. While the others were lost in applause, Nikhil followed Krishna with his eyes as he saw her retreat behind the curtain. He decided to follow her and do a little journalistic sleuthing. Backstage, he saw the man with the scruffy boots announce, 'They're breaking the place down.' And the woman he now knew to be Krishna effortlessly launched herself into the sky. There in the far corner, a jaw had dropped open in the dark of the night. Nikhil Mandal could have had many hypotheses, but this was certainly not one of them. He tried to unlock his phone and turn on the video recorder, but he was too flustered and Krishna too fast.

Krishna hovered over the town square and its fast-crumbling buildings. She turned to the assembled townspeople and urged them to return home and trust her. Nikhil Mandal had scurried his way over and concealed himself in a spot with a vantage point. He watched the townspeople meekly return to their homes; he put this subservience down to people's feudal mindset and their need to be ruled.

Nikhil watched the circus freaks and the hippy man with scruffy boots take front-row seats at the demolition. They sat as if it were a cinema show. It had been a long day. He was hungry and longed to have a shower, eat and watch his favourite show. He contemplated slipping back into the darkness and continuing his intrepid investigations another day, but his journalistic instincts refused this suggestion. He lit a cigarette, promised himself he would take a holiday soon, and sat down to wait. He forced himself to stay awake for the next couple of hours while the wind swamped him with construction dust and Team Krishna's banter and terrible knock-knock jokes. What followed was silence, followed by more idle, meaningless chatter. Nikhil had to wonder what they were doing there and, more importantly, why he was still perched in one place, staring out into the darkness through gritty, fatigued eyes.

Nikhil's tenacity was rewarded after the trucks drove away. The woman with glassy eyes and flowing red hair, in a white costume and gold headband, spoke and instructed the team as if she remembered the exact image of the town square as it was before. A man dressed like he was from the 1500s picked up a pile of rubble as if it were a letter dropped by a pigeon. A dwarf in a three-piece suit freely entered the depths of the earth and emerged from it like a hot knife through butter. Then there was the person whose pigmentationless skin and fierce expression did not warn you of the gentle hands that regenerated all plant life that was squelched just moments ago. As she got to work, he saw her strangely entering plants and becoming one with them, sometimes animating them to reach over and help. And then there was she – the circus leader. She continued to fly and shift buildings like origami figures made out of paper. Together, they worked like a symphony to restore the town square, while the man dressed as if he had stepped off a horse alternately gasped, clapped and pretended to give instructions. 'Hey, good going, guys – one of you might want to get that wall?' Nikhil had seen enough. As the sun started to conquer the dark night, he slipped away, sure in his heart that he would be back soon.

The sun announced its arrival by littering Ujwala with gold beams. The birds sang paeans of praise to its victory. The townspeople began emerging, drawn by their noisy calls. Walking from their homes to the town square - they could not believe what they were looking at for the second time in twenty-four hours. They wondered if they had woken from a nightmare. Otherwise, how else could everything be the same as before? In the melange of people, someone started to clap. It caught on like a yawn, and before long, it turned to thunderous, joyous applause.

Rathore hated thinking old age was making him forget things. 'We saw it being brought down, or was that too much whiskey?' Hussain tapped him on the shoulder reassuringly. 'It wasn't the whiskey.' Gupta whispered what he knew to be true, 'That Krishna had something to do with this.'

Vijendra Gupta awoke expecting the sounds of wailing and complaining; instead, there was an ovation. He was alarmed at seeing a completely intact town square, only with more resplendent vegetation.

Atmaram Gupta looked at his avaricious son and felt a twinge of parental love that was quickly quashed by feelings of disappointment and betrayal. 'Well, son, the creative force is bigger than the destructive one. Let's just say it's a miracle.'

Vijendra Gupta wanted to send a snarky retort back in his father's direction, but he was already thinking about how he would explain this to Lobha. Why couldn't ruining a town be easier? The world was an unfair place.

Chapter 14

The Plot Thickens

Sleep is dispensable. Sex is inconsequential. Food is fattening. Only losing control is unbearable. Give me violence, give me confrontation, but not this. Not this.

Tamas Lobha was worried! It added roughness to his existing coarse persona. He smoked continuously even as the others in the room wheezed. He puffed and snorted and gargled his phlegm – he wasn't having a good day, and he didn't care who knew it. He leaned forward as one of his many assistants attached a hard drive with the available CCTV footage to the oversized screen. It started with images of the demolition – buildings breaking, people crying yade yade ya, and then destruction. 'Go on forward – keep going,' he ordered coarsely. The images sped past, and nothing seemed to change. The screen was a monotonous blur of brown and grey dust. And then there was a flash of light, like a shooting star. Infinitesimally small and quick, it made its way across the horizon, but Lobha's keen-to-win eye caught it: 'Stop, stop, stop – go back.' The visual scurried backwards, stalled and played. Lobha squinted as Ryan carried a gigantic light in and flooded the area. He then proceeded to replace a fallen wall like it was a book on a shelf.

Lobha was still trying to compute Ryan's superhuman strength, when Krishna flew in. His brain circuitry seemed to collapse, and a fog eclipsed it. Nothing in his life had prepared him for what he saw, and he had been around the world and back. Another part of his brain watched as a team of circus freaks worked in tandem and performed non-human feats, and his brain fell into a dissociative fugue. Lobha was used to knowing. And he accepted that control was everything, but here he was in a territory where he knew nothing and could therefore control nothing. How was it even possible? His brain, in shutdown mode, threw up an abstract solution: *Perhaps just charming Krishna would work. I mean, look at how women are so charmed by me!* He looked around at the women in the office with plastered smiles and pleasing ways, and he knew what he had to do. After all, what women ever really wanted was the attention of a powerful man like him.

I would step forward and stand dangerously close to Krishna. Then I would put on my best, most charming smile and whisper in her ear while stroking her arm, and say assertively: 'Look, you're too beautiful to be trapped into doing something like saving the world. Let me take care of you.'

Lobha wanted to savour this moment. He decided to lean back and rest in this new, inspired thought. What a brilliant outcome. He could have his cake and eat it too. But then, even in his mind, all hell broke loose.

Krishna lifted Lobha with one hand, and a storm raged through his office. The gale became vicious, and everyone had to hold on to something. Those who could not floated up like paper bags. He could see his posse hovering and suspended, and he screamed, 'Put me down! Lower me.'

Krishna asked in return: 'Lower than you already are?'

Lobha had seen enough; so he pulled the plug on his mind's eye. He came to his senses as he watched those around him as if they were looking at a mentally unstable person. There and then, he decided to play it the only way he knew – dirty.

MM was fast asleep when his phone rang, but he had a special ringtone for times like these – the National Anthem. You see, it forced him to stand at attention for his boss, no matter the time or place. He did not need more than the first line to go from prone to perpendicular. 'Hello … at you service of your.' Lobha decided he did not care about his word jumble and simply ordered: 'Set the circus on fire.' That felt more like it! Satisfied, Lobha decided to call it a day. Mukesh Mehta was now awake and satisfied at having received his next task. He was so grateful that Lobha kept his sense of purpose alive and his pockets overflowing. A sigh escaped his lips as he prepared not to sleep the night.

Bees in the moonlight look like drops of honey with wings. And this is why checking on them before he turned in for the night was Satya's favourite way to put a bow on the day. But tonight, there was something even better. Krishna joined him and lit up his whole world: 'This is beautiful. Do they sleep at night?'

Satya drew out a tray, and they gazed at the tiny, magical creatures. They continued to buzz, unaware that their existence was linked to the survival of humanity. 'Some of them do, and some don't sleep.'

They stood still, looking at the bees, but their thoughts had moved on. Satya took Krishna's hand, and they looked at each other as if it were for the first time. It was Krishna's first kiss, and it felt just right. It was how she had imagined it would be. For Satya too, this was a first. He had never kissed anyone who had time travelled or could fly or … *Oh, to hell with it*, he thought. Satya wanted to make a move grandiose enough for a superhero. He scooped up Krishna in a sweeping motion, but it had the contrary effect as Krishna took flight and looked down at Satya, who stood with his hands extended as if begging for alms. It took Krishna a moment to realise it was a gesture of love. She gingerly settled back into his arms, but still hovered, giving only the impression of resting in his arms.

'Come on, I can handle your weight,' he said, and Krishna cautiously eased into his arms as they entered his home.

Chapter 15

Where Do We Go from Here?

It is $C_8H_{11}NO_2$ + $C_{10}H_{12}N_2O$ + $C_{43}H_{66}N_{12}O_{12}S_2$. *So Dopamine + Serotonin + Oxytocin = LOVE. If love is nothing but a chemical reaction, then why does it feel both like a splendid thing and a knife in the heart? Why does it feel like a free fall to an unknown destination? The body sings, and the mind floats while one has to still function in the world. The best solution then is to pick something to do that takes you closer to the one you love.*

The build-up to an impending drama involves a series of mundane events. The dominoes fall unrecognised, gaining their significance only in retrospect. Like Satya inviting the children to look through his telescope at the spangled tapestry that hung in the sky because he knew that Krishna would be at the very spot he chose for them to stargaze.

Krishna stood near but was afar as she gazed up, feeling belittled by the mission that refused to elevate itself beyond reconstructing buildings. She frowned at the sky as if asking its residents what the hell they were up to.

Satya had one eye on the frown on Krishna's face, and the other was on the children who jostled for the eyepiece. Satya gently pried them apart: 'Let's do this by turns. That there is The Great Bear.'

Rumi was convinced that no one deserved the telescope more than him. He jammed his face to the eyepiece hard enough to risk leaving an outline similar to a pirate's patch on his eye, but that was no concern to him as he exclaimed, 'Wow … wow …

wow …' With each 'wow', he managed to convince all the others that he was privy to something no one else could see. Satya smiled as he asked, 'What do you see, Rumi?' He knew that Rumi had pressed his eye in too firmly to see anything. Still, he wasn't going to admit it: 'Many, many, many worlds!' With that, another garrulous exchange started amongst the children, and they didn't notice the arrival of Maya, Anita, Ryan and Prince. However, Satya spotted the familiar formation and sighed – things were about to get interesting.

The grass on the field, ignorant of schemes, joyfully rustled in the moonlight – a witness to the townspeople who had assembled at its periphery to seek Krishna's help. Atmaram set his walking stick down on the field and led the march towards the circus. Behind him, Devendra Singh Rathore, Amir Hussain and his wife Rabia followed. While their flashlights alternately lit and lost the path, their conversation and laughter held steady with the years of acquaintance and trust. That was until the air seemed like a fog might be rolling in, accompanied by the smell of torched grass.

Satya's reverie broke with the first scent of trouble. He realised that he could no longer be a bystander to this evolving situation as he saw bellows of smoke rising. There were people from the town out there, and children here.

He watched Anita trying to shepherd them to safety. Still, her knowledge of children's ways was severely limited; so she turned to Jeet for help, who readily stepped up as he announced, 'I'm going into the tent; it will be real fun – anyone wants to come?' That's all it took as they followed the leader.

Krishna took in the aerial view and saw a raging fire enveloping the field. It was growing with ferocity as it raced towards the residents of Ujwala. She spotted the arsonists and Ryan amongst the grass. She felt assured as he moved towards them. There was no better person than Ryan to deal with the miscreants. Ryan, on the other hand, was not so sure.

Chapter 16

Ryan

Over the years, many people have spoken about the truth. For some, the truth can never be hidden. For others, the truth is a set of internal beliefs that need not be revealed. The truth is universal and the truth is subjective. The truth is out there and no one can really objectively see it. So what is the truth? How can one point of view be more true than the other?

The arsonists setting fire to the field seemed to have a sense of purpose. They were dressed in fireproof suits, and plodded through the fields wearing boots and carrying diesel cans. Their conviction and confidence confused Ryan. *Do they realise what they're doing is wrong? And if they knew, from where did they draw this brazenness? What did they imagine was the truth of this situation?* Ryan had always struggled with the chasms between honesty and dishonesty – a space that most of humanity occupied comfortably.

His story was the stuff of folklore, right from the word go. It was AD 1425, and people wondered how a baby his size made it out of his mother without tearing her in half. And so, besides his size, even as a baby, there was myth surrounding Ryan's superhuman strength. Soon, he became a draw for all those in his town, and his legend grew. However, the novelty wore off fast when reality kicked in. As an infant, unaware of his strength, he caused destruction. Not only were there broken chairs and cribs, but there were bruises too. His constant need to feed his fast-growing body led to tantrums that became dreadful for his family. His mother tried to love him, but then her distress took precedence. Ryan went from 'the miracle' to being chained and handcuffed.

He learnt the hard way that, more often than not, he would have to dial back his strength. So, he tempered himself and lived life as if he were walking on eggshells. This also coincided with his establishing a lifelong mission to make people like him. It's about now that Ryan perfected the overenthusiastic smile even when he was offended. He beamed while he seethed.

In his teenage years, his strength became a party trick. They would hoot for him to lift two girls at once, and clap as he pushed horse carts laden with goods. Here too, his strength was a marvel, but only to a point. For example, lifting was fine but dropping and throwing not so much. Pulling was fine, but pushing was comme ci comme ca, and so on. He learnt how to fake his strength, alternating between succeeding and failing to entertain. Every day, Ryan and his wishes belonged less to him and more to those around him. It would seem ironic that the strongest man in the world felt the weakest, but there was no space even for that. Ryan's large frame struggled to fit into the mediocre box of societal structure.

As the years went on, he became the centre of a successful show. He lifted, pushed and dropped with ease while faking effort. Ryan had geared himself to living his lie to the fullest, but he was lonely, isolated and bored. For the ladies, he was an oddity – a handsome beast to be ridden, overcome and captured. They found it hard to love him because they could not see past the large frame that eclipsed the man within. He was extraordinary, and he hated it. Ryan often sat by the window of his room and just envied ordinariness. He flamed with jealousy as he watched people live prosaic lives filled with pettiness. Ryan wanted so badly to gossip, argue about things that did not concern him, and set his ego on some simple issue and watch it flame out of control. Most of all, he wanted to belong. He scoured the world from his elevated vantage and could find no one like him. Till Ameena arrived. Until then, only one person stayed doggedly by his side

– his mother. And everyone knew it was not altruism but the money rolling in that kept her there. Love? That was reserved for his father, who had unceremoniously disappeared when he could no longer handle Ryan's growing strength.

His father lived to dominate others, and his mother had yielded to his every patriarchal diktat. He said 'jump' and she only asked 'how high'. This to her was love – to be metal in the hands of a blacksmith and shaped by his every demanding blow. With Ryan, it was different. What was brewing within his son was an impediment to the father's inflated self-image. And then, quite suddenly, he left, leaving behind Ryan and his older siblings (there were five) and his devastated mother.

Since then, she was constantly present but was never really there. She sat almost motionless – bent, her eyes set to the floor in deference to the moment her husband might return and complete her. She stared down at the stained, wooden surface with widening cracks while addressing her fast-growing child and told him he would have to take care of her and the family. And that is what he did. He and his mother travelled from town to town, displaying his 'enormous' strength without a word exchanged. Ryan continued to stare out at the rambling countryside and looked for the opportunity to smile at anyone who would look his way, not realizing that it left them befuddled because they expected strength to be combined with brutish brusqueness for it to be counted as strength at all.

It was at one such show that he spotted Ameena. She was the tallest girl he had ever seen, perhaps because that is what she was – the tallest girl in the world. Ryan was strong, too strong; and Ameena was tall, too tall. So tall that the proportions of her body were at odds with her exceptional frame – it made her face very long, her limbs extended endlessly and her bones chose to randomly protrude. People looked at her with derision and awe. The strange response she elicited made her withdraw, her face expressionless because she had figured out that no one went that far up or looked that closely. She played with body language to amuse those who came to be entertained by her. She stood nine feet above the ground. Her gangly, misshapen body bowed to enter spaces and stooped to stay there. She bent over further than she needed to, pretended to bump her head on the ceiling and struck her hands on the walls to convince the others that her limbs were too long to be controlled. Ryan listened to the response from the crowd and recognised the 'ooohs' of awe, but then there were sexual innuendos, mocking and some poking with sticks too. It would seem that Ameena was above it all, but Ryan could see that she was not. She was drowning in sorrow and rejection.

They met outside her trailer – Ameena sat a few steps lower – and they talked under the cover of darkness. Hesitantly and slowly, they told their stories, never mentioning the wrongs done to them because that was understood. Ameena told him about the Grand Bazaar and the qawwalis that rang through it. Ryan told her about the best goulash he had ever eaten. They spoke about what they wanted their world to be, and discovered it was the same thing – they wanted it to be simple and ordinary. A few meetings later, a strange colour appeared on Ameena's face; it was the flush of being seen by a man she had only met in the dark. What they saw in each other transcended their physicality. They even held hands, and Ryan gallantly offered to lift her, but she politely declined. They sat, raising their mismatched hands towards the moon's rays, trying to memorise the contours and lines on their palms. Ryan felt something rising within him, and she felt something settling. They waited for the shows they abhorred to end, for the sun to set, and for their meetings. At night, they would find each other, but by day, it was another story. Ameena sat perched on the ledge of her emotions, waiting for them to fly into Ryan's heart.

On the other hand, Ryan was afraid, bound by the same question that marked every endeavour in his life – *What will people think? What will they say when they see two freaks together? What will the world think when they see strongman Ryan with a gawkish, misshapen Ameena?* In answer to these questions, as the sun shone upon them, he looked away even as Ameena tried to catch his eye.

A few years passed, and their nocturnal meetings were tinged with Ameena's sadness. Ryan tried to push past it when he ought to have addressed it. He tried to smile his way out of it, but to no avail. Ameena's unseen eyes incessantly asked: 'Why am I not good enough in the day?' And then she stopped coming, preferring to lie down on the long, hard plank that was her bed and pretend to sleep. Ryan felt her fading away. He had all the strength in the world, but it was not enough to push back his years of conditioning – people must be pleased.

It is a biological fact that taller people tend to live shorter lives. It has to do with the number of cells and their replication. The more there are, the more work the body needs to do. And Ameena was not just tall; some would say she was a giant. Plus, she was underfed and neglected. The shock of realising that time had run out made Ryan's dilemma redundant and froze him in a way that he could not explain. He felt what he had never felt before – self-hate. Ryan's mental self-flagellation took on a life of its own. It became his default mode. He wished he had told her he loved her; he wished he had brought her home and maybe even married her. He wished, he wished, he wished. He blamed himself for Ameena's death, for her unhappiness and for his inability to stand up to society's brutal eye. And the smile from his face receded like a river in hot summer. It first left his eyes, then his angular cheeks, and finally forfeited the mouth to be replaced by the grimace everyone wanted to see. Ryan finally became the brute. He grunted, scowled and frowned fiercely, but it was because he could no longer bear to smile. Inside him, gentleness waited for a receptacle. All he wanted was to go back in time and love Ameena, love her deeply and entirely. But that wasn't possible.

Time was not bendable or stretchable, and certainly couldn't go backwards or forwards.

Then Krishna came along, telling him she had travelled time, saying he could and should use his full strength to save humanity, and he jumped at the opportunity like a thirsty man at water.

He could, at long last, live out his entire truth. As he met the others in the team, he realised that his strength was not just an aberration but a superpower. Ryan believed in Krishna and felt assured that time was indeed elastic. There was hope. Maybe he could love Ameena the way he ought to have.

Now here he was, on his first mission, with the mandate to hurt another human being for real for the very first time. Ryan felt doubt and conflict return. Those self-assured, fire-starting arsonists thought they were doing the right thing. How was he different from them if he hurt them? *I mean, what would they think?* Ryan looked up and spotted Krishna hovering expectantly. She was depending on him, and he was frozen.

It took Atmaram's screams to break him out of the bind. He knew he had to right the balance if the choice was between one unarmed man and a group carrying weapons. Ryan moved in and tossed the arsonists like they were tennis balls. As they scurried away, bruised and scared, he finally accepted his life mission – he would always look out for the weak. He had never known so much peace.

Vijendra Gupta watched Ryan go through a group of practised arsonists as if they were toys and decided to stay on a conveniently placed perch on a tree, far away from harm. From there, he watched the shapes of people silhouetted against bellowing smoke and did not plan to move or care – until it dawned on him that both his son and father were in the way of the blaze. He jumped down and painfully twisted his ankle. Still, he hobbled as fast as possible and ran straight into Maya.

Chapter 17

Maya

They always come in pairs. Like avarice and fear. Jealousy and rage. Or joy and love. There are so many things to learn from minds. Which is why I like getting in there as often as possible.

Maya looked at Vijendra Gupta's contracted pupils and saw a space to dive in. Minds were her playground. She was unsure whether she was born with the power to get into people's heads or if her circumstances forced her to summon up the power to do so.

Maya was an only child for the first eight years of her life. It was the 1960s – an intoxicating time when material prosperity became a real possibility. With it came hedonism. Many self-serving individuals inhabited the earth at this time, and her parents claimed their distinctiveness fiercely. To them, Maya was *a* child, not their child. They believed they were merely her portals into the world. This idea could have translated in many ways but, for Maya, this is how she came to be acquainted with neglect. There were long silences, some constant berating and loud voices in the next room. Looking back, she wondered how a toddler could imagine suicide while not understanding what it was. In her bid to connect with others, she tried to break into their minds. Or was it that she did it because she could? As a child, she mistook these excursions for her imagination, and blamed herself for what she found there. Yet, she scoured for a mind that could show her what she craved – love and faith.

And then she was born. That baby was her sister, but felt like her child. It was love at first sight. There was her beautiful face, thick dark hair, broad forehead, full lips, the tiny upturned nose which changed its mind later and regally marched beyond the proportions of her perfect face. And those beautiful eyes seeking her love and protection launched a promise of premature maternity in Maya's heart. She invoked in Maya the realisation of what she had sorely needed growing up and could now make true for someone else. They named her Mo because her amused parents thought she mewed like a cat. But for Maya, she was a bright star – Mo than enough for her. She had the unique ability to draw love towards herself. She did what no one had done before – she taught her parents how to care. They did as best as they could. Maya watched closely and rushed in to fill any gaps. Secretly, she adopted Mo and promised never to neglect her, always to protect her and not to allow her to feel alone. But then … she hadn't … couldn't keep her resolve.

After the debt collectors killed their parents, in one stroke, she lost her mother and father, her home and all material resources. But she had Mo, and she held on to her as a bridge to life and her reason to believe. They shuffled from relative to a distant relative, from abuse to neglect and back again to abuse. In one of these troughs, she discovered she had a way into minds. She saw images and heard the voices of the owners of these thoughts. At first, Maya blamed her past traumas for what she saw – it was darker than a closed grave and murkier than a cesspool. People kept hidden within them reservoirs of hate and fear, and from it sprung forests of restlessness and looming desires. In those moments, she turned to Mo, where dwelt such faith and belief that it allowed Maya to go on. In Mo's mind, goodness, joy and jokes were trying to take root, and Maya wanted to feed those saplings. And against all odds, she held Mo's sense of joy in her protection, keeping away all the shrunken hearts surrounding them.

Then one day, a fostering uncle came for Mo, and Maya stood between them. The violence that ensued was unusual in its ferocity, and Maya's broken body could find no way to retaliate. So she tore past the pain and went for his mind. Not sure what this feeble defence would bring, she did it anyway. To her complete astonishment, the man who struck her with such certainty was nothing but a bundle of fear, drowning in emotional mayhem. His strong body was not supported by a matching mind. He was mentally cowering. Armed with this knowledge, Maya looked into his darting eyes and forced his body to become one with the cowardice that dwelt in his mind. His hands dropped to his sides, and his trembling legs brought him down to his knees. Maya was seventeen, and Mo was nine, and that's when they became free. Maya had a weapon, and she would use it – after all, what is more frightening for an abuser than to be found out and exposed for the world to see who they are? Mo smiled and leaned into Maya's embrace. She was happy to be enveloped in her sister's care, and Maya rested in the thought that they would always be safe.

Maya quickly understood that fearful minds opened up to her like rain-laden clouds to the earth. The stream was continuous and strong. She previewed mind after mind and understood its true nature, but her findings were disappointing. Minds are circular, automatic and overpopulated with mundaneness. Inside people's heads is a conveyor belt full of paltry issues that they use as lifeboats to make sense of a life that refuses to bow to their barrage of cravings. Like passengers on a train searching for a destination, they move from one vestibule of desire to the next. We imagine our movement causes the scenery to pass, completely forgetting that the train we're on is heading in just a single direction. For some, the destination beyond the trap of their repetitive thoughts is desirable but daunting, but for most these thoughts are their entire reality. And to a few other people on earth, deep silence seems far less exciting than the mental movies that they create daily. The rare ones with clarity have either a larger purpose or an intense personal desire that propels them out of the quicksand of commonplaceness. Either way, minds were burdens that people carried. It was impossible with or without them.

For a few years, this knowledge enabled Maya to live with Mo in the sanguine depths of a superiority complex, thinking she 'knew', and so she had conquered. But that was only partially true. Maya did manage to steer their life to the point of material stability, and it seemed like they could live happily ever after. On the face of it, she was just a woman behind the counter selling ice cream while her sister went to college, but her occasional fortune-telling gigs brought in the jam for the bread she was putting on their table.

Mo became her joy, and she watched with pride as she pirouetted through life with the assurance that falls were for catching. She knew her mess would be cleaned up; so she made one or two. She borrowed money and bought expensive meaningless things. She filled her life with inane activities that she loved – coffee in cafes, beauty parlour visits, costly handbags and luxurious manicures. When Maya asked her what she wanted to be, she answered she wanted to marry rich. At the time, Maya laughed. Mo and Maya always met at the cross section of bad jokes and a weird sense of humour. They laughed even as no one else comprehended their banter – they did not mind.

Maya kept her foray into minds a secret. Mo knew her sister had some extraordinary power, but never enquired about its exact nature. She was growing up and had an evolving life independent of her older sister. It made Maya simultaneously happy and anxious. She was never sure if her baby would make it out in the world. There was no choice; so she bit the bullet and let her go. Now Maya wondered if she should have done that.

Maya's knowledge of people's minds made her distrust most of them; but she was getting lonely, and she succumbed to the promise of friendship with a group of girls considered popular. It was the enticing lure of being a part of a set that did not readily admit others. Maya wanted to fit in; so she traded secret for secret.

Except that it was an unfair trade-off. Needless to say, word got out, and spread it like wildfire. Maya became a novelty with newspapers reporting on her and she was even a minor celebrity. Maya rode the wave and enjoyed the coasting. Somewhere along the way, she lost track of Mo, who found a man and hung up her pretty pirouetting shoes. Maya had presumed that life would always be like that. This, despite knowing its delicate nature and that life doesn't even exist outside people's minds.

Then it was that a great disease escaped from tongues of Komodo dragons and breathed into the lungs of human beings – a sickness that moved from animals to human beings, and had no known cure. Suddenly it was that the earth was smeared with disease and death. Maya wondered if Mother Nature had read the collective human mind like her. Had human minds laden with fear, in fact, pushed Mother Nature to make them come true? 'You want fear?' she asked, and made their worst nightmares come alive. But Maya felt she was set apart from it, above it even. She believed her power made her see through what was at play, and that her knowledge protected her.

Then the sickness caught Mo.

Not a day … not a moment goes past when she doesn't have to stop herself from thinking about the moment she learnt about it. Her utter helplessness as she saw the sickness tear through Mo. And then came the moment when she knew she was gone. Maya knew well that birth and death were figments of minds but her 'knowing' could not stop the loss from possessing her. She knew pain from childhood abuse and neglect. She was acquainted with betrayal because it was the ones closest to her who inflicted the pain. She became conversant with sadness when those in whom she ought to have found shelter abandoned her again and again and again. She even knew reconciliation when she accepted the frailty of human relationships. Then what was it she felt every day since Mo was gone? There was no way to explain the senseless loss.

There were no words to describe the void. There was just a gaping hole of the meaningless. She refused to cry – tears are for those we lose. Mo was not. And so Maya summoned and channelled all her powers and shook the basis of earthly reality. She shook matter and its existence like a snow globe and chased after the floating specks of energy, and rode them to the bridge between life and death. It stood on the tail of a violet light that would carry the dead to the afterlife.

She found Mo on the tip of the purple beam. She had dumped her body and was now lithe, pixie-like, in the colours of the rainbow and turning like a dervish caught in the wind. She seemed to be celebrating. She smiled at her sister with enough love to fill every human heart but did not attempt to speak to her. It seemed that all she wanted to do was to dance in her new-found freedom and slip away as soon as possible. Maya spoke from her heart, 'You, my darling girl, are joy, radiance and beauty. If you could see the crowds of people whose hearts resound with your absence, you would see exactly how special you are. Come back. *Please* return.' For a moment, the whirling subsided, and Maya had the illusion that perhaps she could wrest Mo from death. Mo asked in a whisper, 'Is that who I am?' Maya could only nod vigorously. Then the beam Mo stood on seemed to rev up as if getting ready to shoot off. 'What must I do with those who wait to welcome me on the other side? Shall we leave them sad?' A ripple of anticipation went through Mo as she spoke those words, and Maya understood that she had some other place to be. The next stop on her journey was looming. Mo then turned and pirouetted with a spring in her step one last time, planted a big kiss on her forehead and speeded away while Maya shouted, 'Find me, Mo. Find me, find me, Mo; find me.' She was never sure that Mo heard her; and then she was gone, leaving in her wake a riot of colour and beams of light. Maya's mind was imprinted with the desire to have Mo back. She now had her own cycle that had her chasing the same thought as a dog would its tail. She was permanently trapped in the pursuit of undoing what happened. After that, life lost some meaning for Maya. On one hand, she lost Mo; on the other, found fame.

For those who watched Maya closely, her rising popularity brought the possibility of answers to age-old questions about anatomy. Humanity knew every nook and cranny of the brain, but no matter how deep they delved, they could never place the mind. And Maya knew the mind like the back of her hand; so they presumed she knew where it was. It started with kosher investigations as some questions were asked, and Maya answered as honestly as she could. Soon, curiosity escalated into paranoia. People hold their shame deep in their minds. There, it festers and becomes an unacceptable impulse that they fight. Maya had access to that war, and they couldn't allow it. They drugged her to discover ways to harness her power. They strapped her to a chair. When she screamed, they gagged her. And when she would not stop struggling, they sedated her. As the tranquiliser spread through her body, she felt relief. Her mind, the power to meander into people's minds, plus her lonely life and Mo's swirling memories, had become a burden she could no longer bear. She was happy to slip away into a drug-induced gooey mass of numbness.

Krishna found her just in time and became a saviour in more ways than one. There is a finality to death that is hard to face. It wasn't the prospect of a better world that drew her to Krishna's team; it was the hope of having her sister back. Krishna had Maya at 'I'm a time traveller'. While they were on the topic of 'de-wronging' history, she had some of her own to take care of.

Naturally, she heartily accepted Krishna's invitation and even learnt to love and flaunt her power.

Today, as Vijendra Gupta quaked, Maya saw an open field and prepared to dive right into his mind. He did not know what was exactly wrong but he felt invaded. It made him uncomfortable but he could not stop it. A desperate Gupta decided to throw a punch. He put his weight behind it but it was ill-timed and poorly conceived. He missed, lost his balance and fell at Maya's feet.

The flames raced as Satya tried to outrun them while taking the townspeople with him. They neared the circus but soon realised that Atmaram Gupta was not with them. Satya was torn between getting the others to safety and saving Atmaram. He stood in limbo, watching the flames make their way to the circus and simultaneously engulf the field.

Chapter 18

Prince

There's more going on under the surface than above it. It's not just still waters that run deep. Reality is always underneath; above is only the facade. Below, there is a whole world of its own – bubbling lava, gushing fresh water and creatures who never need light. And the best part is that there are no human beings there.

Prince saw Satya frozen with indecision. He made a choice and dug a ditch deep enough to break the spread of the fire. He was on his way to his happy place as he barrelled through the earth that rushed past him like scenery on a highway.

Prince had a distinct memory of his birth and the dark, sticky, restrictive and somewhat hostile womb that he had to make his way through. He desperately wanted to get out and away from it. So, he pushed harder and harder. It seemed like an eternity until he could see the light at the end. However, when he made it out, he discovered he was still in a dark and muggy canyon. Prince was born in 1932 in a gorge called Patal Kot in the centre of India. Patal Kot received just two hours of sunshine a day. For the rest of the day, a dense fog eclipsed it. Days and nights merged here, visibility was low, and it felt like living under the ground. It wasn't a comfortable place, but the tribe of Patal Kotis lived with a sense of purpose given to them by a legend. Patal Kot was said to be the doorway to the nether world, and the inhabitants its guardians. Their pride in being gatekeepers between life and death made them surprisingly arrogant, although not entirely without mental illnesses caused by the lack of sunshine.

Prince was born to a mother who had no will to live. It was an affliction, not a choice, and the last thing she wanted was to give birth to more life. Prince believed this reluctance made it into her womb, and he contracted it. He was born with limbs shorter than his torso, carrying the rejection in his bones. The proud people of Patal Kot found it hard to love him, and his mother seldom noticed him. Prince spent his time with his body pressed against the earth, engulfed by the opaque mist, and often fantasised about entering the nether world. He did not understand then that his imagination was the precursor to his ability, until his attempts to dig the earth began to yield disproportionate results. His new-found sport meant that Patal Kot became a museum of ditches. Naturally, this did not go down well with the residents, which further alienated him from his community.

On a misty morning, when he was ten years old, his parents made their way out of Patal Kot and into the city. Prince was overwhelmed by the strangeness of it. Never had he seen such bright sunshine dancing on everything around him, making the colours jump and pop. The objects that glistened in its glow beckoned him. He was enchanted by the hustle and bustle, and did not notice when his parents abandoned him. He was an outsider in a strange place. He did not know their language or syntax – or really anything at all. He had no one to turn to and nowhere to go bearing the baggage of sadness he brought all the way from Patal Kot. The only sympathetic creatures he could find were dogs on the street. He joined their pack and helped them bury bones and create crevices to keep them cool and safe. They, in turn, protected him and kept him warm. There was love, friendship and food. Prince could have lived that way forever, but destiny has its ways.

A travelling circus came by and saw Prince rolling with the canines and thought he was amusing. They picked him up and trained him. He was prodded and poked to perform. And perform he did with great aplomb. On display were his height and lack of social skills. He wasn't as wild and certainly not as stupid as they made him out to be. Still, the audience laughed and laughed and laughed – not with him but at him. Ultimately, it got to him, and he dug deeper than he had ever before, even while fearing that he might never find a way out.

It is here that Krishna found him. Now, at Krishna Circus, Prince had everything he had ever longed for – respect, family and now maybe love. He thought about Maya, and it warmed his heart to about the same degree as the earth around him.

Prince pummelled through as quickly as possible, and when he emerged, he had managed to dig a small ravine between the fire and the people of Ujwala. Near the circus tent, a cheer went up even though they did not fully comprehend the turn of events that saved them.

Satya could not join the celebration with the knowledge that Atmaram would not make it. He prepared to mourn the loss till he spotted Krishna above him.

He saw her hesitate – not the best time to mentally debate if it was the right time to reveal her identity, but that's what she seemed to be doing. A blazing fire was getting too close to Atmaram. With some relief, Satya realised she had decided against any further contemplation and got in there. She swooped down and, in one move, took Atmaram out of harm's way and into the sky.

'Do superheroes always have to cut it so fine?' Satya mumbled to himself as he rushed back into the tent to join the celebration.

Atmaram, suspended in Krishna's arms, was happy to have his hunch confirmed, but his vertigo prompted him to close his eyes and he only felt the air whistling in his ears. Krishna set him down near his home and nodded at him: 'Stay safe.' Atmaram wanted to say something but only managed an 'I knew it, I knew it'.

Krishna was tempted to attend to Atmaram's euphoria but had other urgent matters to take care of. She reached the river and moved a column of water with her baton while neatly marking an area for it to contain itself – as if she were drawing a square using chalk on a blackboard. She made her way above the flaming field and dropped it with force. To those watching from the circus windows, it looked like God sent torrential rain.

Vijendra Gupta was not sure if he was relieved or horrified. Maya saw that his tortured face was no match for the giant demons that inhabited his brain – his avarice and hunger for money and power, and the utter contempt for humanity that was thriving there. Also, within him lurked a child who wanted to outshine his father. Maya retreated out of his mind and decided that Vijendra was his own worst enemy and watched as he limped away as far as he could from her.

Chapter 19

Anita

Gender. One word that has caused only confusion. A human-made construct that denies the continuum on which all of nature lives. The unending variations that make Earth beautiful cannot be put into categories. Why do humans love boxes? This attempt to understand life by organising it into classifications is rather useless. It only serves to erase the essence of life – constant change that signals us to go with flow. Those from the plant kingdom understand this well.

It was a new day as Anita emerged from Krishna Circus and stretched lightly. Although nervous, she wore a little smile as she looked forward to the beautiful morning ahead. She stepped on to the field that was reduced to cinders. Grey flecks of ash floated in the air and stuck to her face and hair. She brushed them off gently as one would a minor admonishment, even as the ground seemed to suck her bare feet into squelchy grey mud. No, she did not mind one bit. In death, she saw life, and she had seen death in plenty.

She closed her eyes and went back to a time ahead – to 22 May 2090. It was past midnight. Anita was deep asleep in the room she shared with her brother. Some would say they were soulmates. He was older than her, and she looked up to him. He was the gentlest man she knew, and the least judgemental. Growing up, her physical development was unusual; but if he noticed, he never commented on it. He accepted her as she was. No changes and no justifications required. Anita wasn't the only one who admired him; he had a hero-like quality that drew people to him. It was a marvel for her to watch him at the centre of groups, even though he did not tick even a single box of how leaders of packs were supposed to be. He had neither a grandiose air, nor ever thought of anyone as below him. No matter who it was, he stood as an equal with them. It did not make a difference that the plummeting, vitiated environment on Earth had made his skin sallow, and he had lost his hair at an early age. He was terribly allergic to the pollutants and could only really survive indoors.

That night, the air outside was particularly unbreathable. The oxygenator hummed through their home, providing them vital clean air. Was it a natural way to live? Of course not. Human beings, like frogs in hot water, did not notice that the heat from a fire that, ironically, they had started, was being turned up. In their sweet self-denial, they thought they were skirting its domino effect even while being one of the dominoes. And then the last piece fell in Anita's hometown. She vividly remembered the smell that carried this news through the ducts and spread like a rumour through the house. An unbearable stench that felt as if it had been mined from the depths of hell. There was no smoke or fog, just the ever-growing stink that seemed to envelop them like an invisible prison. It was her brother who first coughed in his sleep, and then the putrid air assaulted Anita's chest. Sounds of heaving lungs trying to fight for their lives filled the house. They gathered in the living room, searching each other's watering eyes for a solution.

Anita's parents had taken their time getting used to her, what they liked to call, 'inbetweeness'. Anita's body had both male and female genitalia but her soul was feminine. Her brother's total acceptance of her finally nudged them to do the same. Soon, they forgot to look at their children as belonging to any category and just got down to simply loving them.

They were a family, in the real sense. They talked about everything, helped each other all the time, and truly admired each other, and so, in time, they became a single unit, hardly needing anyone from outside. That night, synchronically, all four of them wanted to delay bedtime. And so they decided to play a game of Scrabble. It was a game that served everyone. Her father was good with words; Anita always managed to pull the best letters. Her brother opened the board and her mother, who hated losing, invented words and insisted they were real. One of them was *garbari*, which she said meant a girl who makes trouble in the best possible way. Another one was *puchkee*, meaning the most beloved child in the whole world. They did try to convince her otherwise, but of course, she refused to listen. They laughed and, as usual, accepted her imaginary vocabulary. This interplay of love and acceptance was the real reason they played the game. And then, as usual, they ate too much ice cream and went to sleep when they could no longer keep their eyes open.

Now, as they stood squinting and gasping while trying to adjust the oxygenator, Anita opened the door and led them out to get away from the room that was turning into a gas chamber. When they stepped out, the apocalypse was in progress. No matter how many science fiction films she had seen, Anita was not prepared. The hacking sound of people trying to catch a breath, distressed family members crying out in pain, and the now opaque air that enveloped them seemed unreal to Anita. People dropped like flies – their chests clogged, skins aflame, they choked and charred to death. Her father, mother and brother fell almost immediately, their skins receding into their bones as the chemical attacked it; their eyes stunned with pain and mouths no longer able to express it. Her brother raised a hand to his mouth and then extended it in her direction – it seemed to her that he was trying to blow her a kiss. Anita tried to help by pouring water into his mouth, but it only seemed to aggravate his agony. She screamed in shock as she watched her family disappear and leave behind skeletons. The chemical carnage continued till Anita fell to the ground. She vanished into unconsciousness, wracked with the desire to see her family again.

Anita woke up disoriented and unsure if it had been a nightmare until she saw the heaps of disintegrated bodies and wilted plant life. She wondered how it was that she was still alive. Anita was in the vice grip of guilt for surviving what her loved ones could not. They were gone. Her whole world was gone. Mindlessly, she walked through the piles of bodies looking for her family – praying that they had somehow survived knowing they had not. There were only heaps of bones fused tight by the chemicals that looked like misshapen cement blocks, like milestones of death. The whole town was just a messy mass of brownish carcasses strewn where people once walked. Anita could still not fathom how it came to be that she was the only one standing. Perhaps they needed to be revived like she was. Maybe these balls of bones could be untangled. She was going to resuscitate them. She would save them because, without her family, she did not exist. Not knowing where to start, Anita started screaming for help and had the scary feeling that she was alone. Until she saw them.

Metal masks obscuring their faces, they were clearing carcasses as if weeding a garden. 'Can you please help me? HELP! HELP!' she screamed. Their ambling ceased as soon as Anita was in their view. They stumbled away from her as if they had spotted an ogre. She saw their pointing fingers and heard their muffled screams of terror. She could not understand why, until she looked down at her own body.

Anita wondered what she was looking at. What was this pinkish-white substance on her skin? She rubbed her arms to brush it off. She rubbed harder. She scraped her arms on the ground and drew blood, but it remained, as it was, the pale pink. It dawned on her that her skin had been drained of all pigmentation. That's when she joined their screaming with her howls of horror. She ran as fast as her legs could carry her. Looking for refuge, she found a perfectly intact concrete building. The irony of these man-made structures out-surviving their makers didn't quite land on her panic-struck mind. Her body quaked as she rummaged through someone's old belongings to find something to cover herself with and waited. No one came looking for her. Fleeing from what they thought was a ghost, perhaps they had decided not to chase her. Her shivering body reverberated with grief till it became a hum – a tone that was the background score to her life to this date. Living like this was impossible, she decided, and she willed herself to die; but exhaustion forced her into a deep, long, disturbed slumber. She awoke to find her hometown now a wasteland of concrete structures devoid of even dead bodies. There was no longer any trace of life or even death, except the shrivelled plants and trees – their dry leaves whirling in the dust, surrounding her like fireflies curiously flitting about a new being. She dragged herself to the tune of her grief. Tears fell from her eyes and marked the path ahead of her. One minute they were a family sleeping happily; the next, they were gone. The possibility of a different outcome haunted her. She was convinced there had to be another ending – a happy one. But there were not even any dead bodies, or any trace of anything that was once living.

That's when she noticed the hints of a corpse – a dead rose bush. And it happened for the first time. As her grief-ridden hand made contact with the plant, it began to revive – like waking from sleep. It unfurled itself and seemed to raise its head to look at her. Was it she who had brought the shrub to life? How did this happen? Much later, she contemplated what it was that she and the ones with roots had in common – living after death. Of course, they knew it even better than her and were at complete peace with it because death was just a season to them. They bloomed, flowered, bore fruit and then let it all fall away, letting every single leaf go. Never lamenting the lost spring or dreading the oncoming winter, bare-barked, they stood with their roots intact, still reaching for life. In their apparent death lurked resplendent life. And now Anita knew death too. She surmised that the reason for her staying alive was that she believed there was some potential for life. In anguish, she held on to the possibility of living, no matter how much death surrounded her.

Still, none of what she was feeling made sense to Anita until she touched the rose bush. She had found her tribe. They too recognised her as their own. The plants, the trees, the grass and shrubs, all leaned towards her with love, welcoming her home.

Later, Anita tried the same with human beings but never had success. Human beings were trapped in their concepts of life and mortality. They were utterly convinced of the reality of age and the linearity of life. Their minds told them they would traverse life from birth to death, but the journey from death to life was not a full circle they quite understood or believed. The imminent ending of things gripped the human race and all they did was set about trying to halt the march of time. Instead of celebrating erasure as freedom, all they wanted was to stop themselves from being erased.

Somewhere in the wasteland, where all else was destroyed, the surveillance cameras still relayed information.

Inevitably, they came looking for Anita. As they surrounded her with heavy weapons and threats of violence, her powers got another facet – one which was even more powerful. Hiding behind a banyan tree she had revived just days ago, she thought she heard the tree talking. 'Come closer,' it whispered. Anita embraced the tree and felt herself becoming one with its trunk. She had entered the tree and could hear its thoughts. And, miraculously, she could use their branches as her limbs. Anita waited inside the tree, listening to it complaining: 'It's been centuries since I have been standing here and watching human beings wreck the earth. Cutting the branch they are sitting on – how utterly stupid and inconsiderate.' Those sent to capture her scoured the area and, not finding her, they pulled out an electric saw to hack down the banyan tree. Incited by the tree's mutinous talk, Anita used its branches to swat them away. This temporarily stopped them, but she knew they would be back.

To save the forest, she allowed herself to be carried away to a laboratory. The word 'mutant' was said a lot, and she soon accepted the nomenclature. What she could not accept was that proud trees were brought down, delicate creepers were squashed, and plants liberally torn from their roots just so that she could bring them back from the dead. Exactly a year later, on 22 May 2091, tired and depressed by this carnage, she broke away. Anita gathered her courage and her fiercest allies – the plants. They basked in her courage, and together they rained chaos on the facility. They reached through windows and doors as Anita brought their branches in, wrapped their vines around those who tried to stop her, and obscured their vision by getting the plants to lean into each other. Anita was almost successful until she found herself at a dead end on a long white corridor. It could have been the perfect camouflage for her, but she was still trapped.

That's when Krishna found her and she could differentiate a courageous spirit from the walls that matched the colour of her skin. She had saved her. Days later, after Krishna had nursed her back to strength, she heard the story and the mission. It all seemed so far away, like a millennium away.

What made Anita join Team Krishna? Besides having a spot on the team that would save the world, Krishna could, at least potentially, reverse an apocalypse. It was this possibility that was most alluring for Anita, who mentally visited the catastrophe in her hometown daily, and prayed for just one chance to pre-empt it. Anita was grateful just for being saved and being able to save others. But now there was something in it for her too. Perhaps the tent would take them back to that moment and avert the disaster, and she could save her family and plant kin.

Her smile grew wider at the thought. She opened her eyes and got to work. An hour later, the field was again as it always was – golden, green, brown, pink, yellow, red, purple, violet, blue – more green and rustling with life.

Chapter 20

Anti-national

There are people who don't like air conditioning. Do you know who these people are? Those that can have it at any time. There are some people who like to live in nature and the outdoors. Do you know who these people are? Those who only do it for fun. I have been on the side where we had no choices. Now I'm on this side and I'm sure as hell going to make every damn choice I want.

Lobha had acquired state-of-the-art indoor golfing apparatus, and used his gold club to putt a ball into the virtual greens. He was hitting masterstroke after masterstroke while his cronies oohed and aahed. Needless to say, MM was the most voluble. Lobha stepped away and continued swinging the club as if exercising his wrists. The loud swishing denoted that its distance from Mukesh Mehta's skull was just far enough for only luck to stand between him and sure death.

Lobha spoke softly, as if almost to himself, 'I hate when things don't work out. So I make sure they always do.' Returning to the ball, he took a long, hard swing and sent it into computer-generated oblivion. He continued to speak as if there was just him and his inflated ego in the room: 'People love heroes and hate terrorists. And converting one into the other is a job easily done.' MM smiled. He understood Lobha like no one else. His boss wasn't a fan of unnecessary smiles; so, to mark the end of the conversation, Lobha flung the club and sent everyone helter-skelter. It amused him, and he laughed as if it was a war cry – a howling that carried down the long hallway, boarded the lift and reached every nook and cranny of WTF, where an eerie silence received it with trepidation.

It was siesta time in Ujwala. The children made their way back from another day at school without a teacher. Others closed their businesses and headed home for a short rest. Yet others stepped away from a morning of idle chatter for an afternoon of silence.

The first explosion shattered the calm. A strange silence followed as people of the town stared at the ripped remains of a central building. It seemed that the people in it had been saved by their rigorous need for an afternoon siesta. It was a few minutes before they realised what had caused the explosion, but could still not comprehend who was behind it.

Eka heard the blast in the distance and, from the voices of the adults, she could tell that they must make their way to safety. With Jeet's help, Eka led the others to the top of the hill. But Rahul was unable to keep pace, and Rumi and Dhwani were distracted. That's when the second bomb went off. The explosion narrowly missed Rahul, Eka and Jeet, but Rumi and Dhwani caught some of the flying debris. It was Eka who found her voice and used it to call upon the others for help.

Hospital waiting rooms are prosaic places designed to discourage germs and emotions – fluorescent lighting, white floors, matter-of-fact grey chairs facing a large TV playing headlines on a loop. Sitting in rows that faced the same way, no one needed to be face-to-face with worry or distress.

Dhwani's and Rumi's parents, the Hussains, were wracked with anxiety as they made small talk over the noise of a blaring television, hoping to normalise a situation they found hard to bear. Thankfully, the others arrived bearing flasks of tea. They passed around cups without exchanging words and watched Ujwala being splashed across the screen. Sensationalist journalists drummed up exaggerated introductions, coupled with confirmed news of Krishna's involvement. It described in every crafted detail her collusion with an enemy state to 'stop development' in India. Words like mercenary, the pieces-pieces gang, outsider, anti-national and then finally terrorist flashed across Krishna's face. They repeatedly struck the 'anti-national' blow, like a hammer on a nail, until it was perfectly entrenched as the truth. And on it, they hung their real intent of sending the army in to get rid of Krishna and take over the field to make more money. It was as convincing as propaganda was known to be, and just as justified. To Amir Hussain, this clever montage seemed like a performance. He would have walked away from it at another time, but could not. There was too much at stake. He was the first to speak: 'It is hard to believe something like this would happen here.'

Priya Mehra took that as a plea for confirmation, and spoke with conviction, 'I knew there was something wrong with them.' Yash Mehra jumped in to support his wife: 'You think it's a coincidence that since they have come, so much trouble has befallen us? Outsiders can't be trusted.'

And so, the baby lie grew to become an indisputable truth. In 2024, there was no shortage of screens and unscrupulous politicians. It was the support of these legislators that gave it legs to run, and today Ujwala was their playing field. The voices on and off the screen grew louder and louder and, within minutes, there was a consensus – Krishna and her team were strangers who had visited horrors upon them. Every setback in their lives and in the town was caused by her and her alone. Krishna was the cause of all their miseries.

In all this, no one noticed the children, Jeet and Eka, who were listening to the adults intently. Worried and confused, they felt a sense of betrayal. They were getting a distinct impression that they had been fooled. They had trusted the bad guys, and now their friends were in danger. Sitting side by side on a hospital bench, they decided they need to take matters into their own hands.

Prince saw the news first, and when Krishna heard the latest nomenclatures, she seemed dispassionate. After all, she was not sure what it all meant. *Wasn't the truth the truth? Wasn't it always victorious? So what was all this?*

Somewhere in her mental landscape, she heard her team's righteous arguing.

Ryan had never imagined that humanity would take their love of falsehood to this extent: 'Doesn't the truth matter any more? How can lies like these be accepted by all?' Maya saw what was in store: 'Yes, they can, and they do. I can tell you it will get a lot worse in the years to come.'

Prince was filled with a feeling of dread. His life before this had been at the mercy of untruths, and he knew how bad it could get. 'We have to stop this now. Do you know they are sending an army in for us?'

Krishna knew they were looking to her for a response, but she was foraging for answers at a time when her mother was still with her. She trusted that Yashoda would have prepared her for this moment. All she needed was to recall the lesson. Closing her eyes, she sat cross-legged on the ground and, much to the dismay of her team, she began to breathe slower and slower until it seemed that she might not be breathing at all. But they understood and waited for her to return from her inner spiritual journey.

It was a cloudy, rainy afternoon in 1770. Yashoda had spent the morning training with thirteen-year-old Krishna. They were in a village in Kerala, India. Krishna was learning Kalarippayattu, the ancient Indian martial art where physical and mental abilities meet to create a form for an indomitable being. Her teacher was none other than Unniyarcha – a woman whose fighting prowess and technique were legendary. Made famous by the direct contrast between her petite frame and her ability to cause severe harm, Unniyarcha soon became an icon. Many wanted to be taught by her, but she accepted only the most worthy. She took Krishna under her wing and taught her to take her body to its full potential. Krishna felt herself connected to parts of her body and mind that she did not even know existed.

One afternoon, the arrival of the monsoon had driven them indoors. Yashoda took the opportunity to educate Krishna on another aspect of combat – how not to be defeated by slander. 'It is to be expected that on your journey, there will be those who will sully your name. However, one who does not identify with one's physical body cannot be tarnished. Remember, Krishna, my dear child – you are not your body. You are spirit. And the spirit cannot be destroyed by a weapon, burnt by fire, dissolved by water, or affected by storms. You cannot be sullied, my dear child. The truth is eternal and thrives within you.'

The words echoed in Krishna's mind as she turned to her team with neither worry nor anger nor pride. But before she could utter a word, Eka and Jeet chose to ambush them. Red-faced with anger, they had what looked like water balloons in their hands. Eka's voice trembled as she spoke, 'You think you're too clever, but we know who you really are!' Jeet added, 'You're a liar. We hate you.' Krishna heard the words but knew it was fear, not hate, and her heart went out to them. 'Hey, come here, let me give you a present and then let's talk?' Krishna's extended hand only served to upset Eka further. 'We don't want anything from strangers.' And before any more words could be exchanged, the duo slipped into the circus, where they proceeded to pelt the facade with two of the four water balloons they had carried.

Anita had spent the better part of the day watching Krishna and her team being vilified and described as hardened criminals. Human beings were stupid because they presumed their superiority. They imagined their minds had no limits when in reality they were confined, small and limited in their outlook. She felt her hate for humanity return, and her body shook with anger that these little human beings dared to bring their ill-informed brains into a place designed to save them. Her rage made her choose the wrong moment to express her feelings of indignity and self-righteousness. She did not know how to punish them, but she would find a way to scare them. 'So you think Krishna is a terrorist?' Anita thought she heard them say, 'Absolutely.'

In a fit of rage, Anita grabbed Eka's and Jeet's hands, and with single-minded ferocity, she dragged them to a painting on the circus wall that, at that very moment, began to howl with images of death and darkness. Anita lost all control and stepped into that whirling horror with Eka and Jeet. Strangely, the tent accepted their attempt at time travel. A moment too late, she realised how ill-conceived this move was as they seemed to be sucked into a long tunnel filled with circles of light. It appeared that it was not they who moved, but everything around them hurtled forward. They could see particles of light swirling and swishing, forming patterns they had not seen before. It was just a moment, but felt like a lifetime. And faster than regret made it from her brain to her heart, they were in a place so pristine, it could only be Kams's kingdom. At that moment, Anita realised the reason for the terrible imagery depicting what lay ahead.

Mistaking it for another circus trick, Eka and Jeet continued to hold Anita's hand. Their fear was quickly replaced with awe. Mathura looked like it had been painted and crafted to perfection, and that's probably because it was! *Wow! Are we in a dream*? Eka wondered aloud. Jeet said, 'This is heaven, Eka, but I don't think we are dead.'

Anita understood how bad it was when Jeet's and Eka's voices pierced the quiet humming of Mathura and made every head turn. If this was indeed Mathura, they were the only children in it, and Anita was their only protector. They came in droves, drawn to a sound that had not been heard there in what seemed like an eternity. Anita was at a loss as flawless beings encircled them, their eyes dripping with envy and curiosity. They bent low as they tried to catch a glimpse of and touch the children, their fingers prodding to feel childhood which was a memory from a distant past. Eka and Jeet stood motionless in the thrall of their mask-like faces. Their lurking, jaded souls pushing at the periphery of their ever-youthful skins, they inched closer until

Anita stood between them. She looked to find a fern, a flower, a tree – anything she could use to protect them. But there was no real plant life in her vicinity.

Time is relative. When you're killing intruders, it flies faster than thought, but when it's waiting for the arrival of a supposed nemesis, it stretches on and on and on … forever. Kams approximated that 'She' would arrive soon through the energy ether. He stared into the empty space and wondered if she might appear right before him. The imagined has more power than the real, and Kams was convinced that, in reality, this augured messiah would be just another story made up by people to keep their hopes up. Maybe she would never come. This thought too brought no comfort. What is dark without light? But he had no time to ponder over that thought because the sweet sound of a loud siren wailing to announce a breach from across time made its way to Kams's ears. He turned towards the sound like a sunflower to the sun. It was a slight movement to mark the moment when Kams realised that she, the saviour was here and he would kill her and live on forever. He was sure that she had come drawn by the deep desire to kill him, and he wanted to seize the moment now!

The screens flickered to life. Kams peered while his heart threatened to beat itself out of his body. But he couldn't find what he was looking for. He saw two of those abhorrent creatures called children and a mutant. Was this mutant She? She who was born in Mathura and who was augured to kill him? She who would 'restore Mother Earth' and diminish his power? Something told Kams that this person drained of pigmentation was not the one … but it was not a complete loss. Krishna herself may not be here, but these things, these creatures, certainly had something to do with her.

In the intervening years, Kams had put his best minds to work to break open the portals, but they were always unsuccessful.

Parshuram, the stubborn fool, did not divulge a thing even though they kept him teetering on death's precipice. It took many years before they discovered the one and only way. If someone from Krishna's time period made their way to Mathura through the portal, they could follow the energy trail back. Since then, Kams had waited every single day. His bet had been on Krishna, but this would also do – bait for the big fish.

Kams felt impatience taking hold of him. He simply could not bear the time it was taking, and he wished he had a faster way to reach his destination.

He kept a keen eye on the flustered trio on the screen in his hovercraft even as he yelled to make it go faster. He was glad to see the mutant and two vermin squirm, and was impatient to turn it into some real pain. Before he could unfurl his fantasies of torture, something changed on the screen. *Was that another person who had pierced the ether? Was Mathura just a thoroughfare for time hoppers?* It took a moment for him to recognise this new entrant. Her blue bodysuit hugging her tall frame, peacock feather adorning her forehead – she looked strong, fearless and formidable – this was the augured one! The one he was waiting for. And she was staring him straight in the eye, even through the screen. Kams knew he had to finish her, or she would indeed do the same to him. He felt a tremor of mortality go through his body and shouted for his hovercraft to go faster.

Krishna had an idea about what was coming and how fast it would reach. And then, within minutes, they would all be dead. With no time to waste, she lifted Anita, Jeet and Eka and, faster than Kams's adrenaline could course through his body, they were once again in the corridor of swirling light and back in Ujwala. They were safe, but the damage had been done. Krishna had imagined it all to be different; she was supposed to chase him, but this would be the other way around. Kams knew the way to Krishna, and he was sure to come after her.

Securely back in the circus and, though thankful the children were safe, Krishna was dismayed that one of her team members had put their lives in danger. And all Anita could come up with was to mouth 'sorry' from a distance. *Was she hoping for forgiveness with that?* Krishna's relief at having them safe outweighed the anger. She brought out a toy elephant – fashioned using rough silk, with tassels and jewels – from the large metal trunk that Yashoda had created for her. It carried a little wand in its trunk. The wand could take you wherever you wished. Krishna was five when little 'Gajoo' was presented to her. Gajoo and the wand had transported her to any place in her imagination – mountains filled with snow, bodies of water, hail, planets of cotton wool – just about any location in her imagination. She handed it to Jeet and Eka, and told them what Yashoda once said to her: 'This is your ride into your imagination. On it, you can go anywhere you like. Load it as high as you want, but it will never heave.' Jeet and Eka accepted the present in a daze: 'Thank you … but who are you? And where did we go?'

For the next hour or so, Anita and Krishna brought Jeet and Eka up to date with the events of their lives so far. The youngsters who had spent much of their lives living in an imaginary world they had created had little trouble believing the story. As yet uncrushed by the weight of 'reality', they soared in the realms of truth and trust. So they could hear what was said instead of going just by the words. Plus, what they had been through needed to have an other-worldly explanation even to make sense. And so, not surprisingly, both understood and believed every word uttered by Anita and Krishna.

They were bursting with a new story to share. Eka and Jeet could no longer amble, and broke into a sprint. The green and brown grass grazed their legs, the insects buzzed in their ears, and they inhaled the fragrance of flowers – it all had a new meaning today.

Giddy with the realisation that the bounty of Mother Earth was what mattered, they reached the hospital holding a bunch of freshly picked flowers and a secret. The flowers went into a makeshift vase, and the secret tumbled out like a waterfall and was received with complete understanding by Rumi and Dhwani. The animated discussions that followed brought the hospital staff into the room. Eka and Jeet were shunted out, but they had successfully transferred their excitement and left their friends with the understanding they needed.

Eka liked to share everything with her parents, and Jeet thought it was his duty to update the adults; so they shared their discoveries with them. But they found the adults too preoccupied with what they were watching on their screens. They just heard another grand story from their children with faked interest and made a mental note to regale others with tales about their children's fertile imaginations. Right now, there were more pressing matters – the army was marching towards Ujwala to tackle Krishna the terrorist and her band of anti-nationals. Theirs was fast becoming the kind of story they had previously loved and devoured through the media.

Chapter 21

Lobha

It's a hard realisation that worrying does not seize whether you are rich or dirt poor. Life has a way of always keeping you on your toes. Even so, it was nicer to worry in a large house and with a seriously massive bank balance.

Sleep had never been his ally. Sometimes he wondered if he got his recommended exercise right here in his bed, what with the amount of twisting and turning he did every night – the rolling around in bed and the arm thrashes ought to count for something! Lobha lay in an oversized bed, with a golden frame encrusted with precious stones he had bought with money he had made himself. It was 2 a.m., and he felt his hands go up to touch the wealth that he lay on, and a feeling of deep satisfaction washed over him. Life was good. Life was where he wanted it to be. For now.

Lobha glanced over at the other side of his bed and, in a beam thrown by the moon, lay perhaps the most perfect woman in the world. Her endless limbs filling the bed from headboard to the footboard, her face was buried in a feather pillow – mouth open, dribbling spots of spit. Her upturned nose honked irregular snores into the room. Yes, it was an imperfection, but Lobha decided it was okay for now, although he couldn't be sure about tomorrow. Love is expedient; lust and love in a Venn diagram would be more like two circles sitting on top of each other, and everyone knows that lust is fickle and ever-changing. But for now, he loved and desired this supple, almost perfect creature. It gave him some solace during these insomniac nights to see how her legs extended way beyond his, but it also reminded him of his imperfections. This yoyo of self-esteem defined his entire life, it went between the world he was born into and raised in and this life now. In his childhood his emotional pendulum swung between his loving mother, who denied him nothing, and his abusive father, who gave him nothing.

The temperature was just right, and he had all the paraphernalia he needed – the silk pyjamas, drugs to help relax him, the most expensive mattress money could buy and no debts that could keep him awake at night. But sleep, it just wasn't for him. The endless chatter in his brain and the sounds of the night kept him company while the world slept. He heard the washing machine downstairs reverberating as it worked to clean stains and felt comforted to know that there was some other live entity besides the two of them in their home – a mansion he had secured so well that prisons would envy it. In this day and age, no one can be trusted. People wanted more and more and more. And they were willing to steal and kill to get what they wanted. Who knew that better than him? These were terms that were set before he decided to live by them. Since he could remember, he heard people talking about goodness, love and equality. But then, under the slightest pretext, they would become discriminatory, hateful and violent. Lobha thought about all the people in the world who were frequent recipients of hate – there were so many – genders, religions, races and castes. It would seem that no one was exempt except those who fiercely clawed their way up the proverbial class mountain. In general, these were wealthy men – Lobha smiled at the thought of being part of this group. Now it didn't matter how he looked, what his social graces were, or that he had zero scruples. They would accept him no matter where he went. He was the master of his destiny, and nothing could stop him. Lobha was coasting on his laurels when the beautiful woman next to him changed her side and broke his stream of thought. Her bare back was in the moon's spotlight. Gleaming like a jewel. Lobha pulled the covers over him, waiting for slumber to come. A little while later, it was

2.30 a.m. and then 2.45, but sleep was still nowhere in sight. So he decided to descend to where the washing machine whirred and the snacks resided.

He swung his legs to the side of the bed and discreetly pulled forward the step he never used when others were awake. Then he just hopped off. Tonight, he elegantly stepped off and made his way down the staircase as he trailed an ornate banister with his manicured hands. He turned left to a room behind the kitchen and found the machine. It had dislodged itself from the designated enclosure and relocated – moved by the force of its motor. It stood leaning against a wall like a punished child, still whirring, as if pleading to be let off. Something about this disobedient machine irked Lobha, and he decided he would throw it out and get a new one the very next day. Even damn machines couldn't be relied on. To hell with them too.

Lobha found another step. This one was sturdy and gleaming, like it was polished only minutes ago. He stepped up to the snack cupboard. There it was, like Ali Baba's cave – such an abundance of junk food. It denoted prosperity to him as nothing else did. Cheese puffs, chips of all kinds, nachos, squishy candy, boiled candy, chocolate, wafers, more chips, heavily buttered popcorn, soda of all types, and an array of instant noodles. He roughly grabbed what he could as if it were a raffle and looked at his bounty – two packets of gummy bears, one of cola candy, tomato-flavoured chips and cheese balls. His hands were full, and he knew he could always return – life was good.

Lobha made his way to the sprawling sofa and drew his iPad to himself with cheeseball-stained fingers. It was only 3 a.m. The snacks spurred a desire to be entertained, and he wondered how the preparations were going. The march to annihilate Krishna and her shabby band should be underway. He dialled MM on a video call. No surprise that MM picked up almost immediately, but something about his subservient sleepy face irritated Lobha, and he disconnected without saying a word.

Lobha then scrolled down his many emails while simultaneously disconnecting all of MM's calls as he desperately tried to call him back. He could bet a bunch of dollars the fool thought he had disconnected by mistake. No doubt he wanted to please him and to be of service to him. Lobha was appeased but still annoyed, and so he decided he would be disconnecting all of MM's calls till he gave up. He also knew that MM would not give up, but he was not one to care.

The email marked 'confidential' was the one he rolled around in his mind like single malt in a ball glass. There it was – a heavy-handed plan to carpet Ujwala with soldiers. March to the circus and imprison its freaks who would find no support because they were anti-national terrorists. Life is simple when you have the might of law enforcement, coupled with a supplicant media. In his mind, he completed what the email did not state: they would then hand over the field to him. He would exploit it and get richer still, and consequently more powerful. The thought consumed him, and he could feel the victory. He stood up, wiped his orange-stained hands on his silk pyjamas, and made his way to his overstocked bar. Grabbing a tall glass, he topped it with some bespoke Rum. He never needed anything to blunt it – no ice, no water and absolutely no soda.

His handprint unveiled a screen from behind a faux bookshelf in his private office. Lobha knew surveillance was the key to control, so he was tapped into the most secure systems worldwide. He was ready for the theatre of war as he prepared to fall into a slumber to the soundtrack of his ascending power. He, Lobha, had enabled, by pushing and ultimately coercing some of the most powerful men in the country to move armies to do his bidding. Lobha would have his way. He would have what he wanted. His greed was their command.

At 6 a.m., he watched as trucks full of army men prepared to leave. It was then that he fell asleep. Even though he knew it wouldn't last long, he embraced it and floated away temporarily.

Chapter 22

The Anatomy of Fear

For some it's breaking a sweat, for others it's quaking knees, or a swirling gripping sensation in your stomach. And then there are the unfortunate ones who had all the symptoms. These ones usually lose bowel control. Look at a person and you can tell how much fear they have. One can read people and use it against them so, so easily. But not for me. I use my own fear before anyone else can.

Greed, avarice, covetousness – who said they are sins? Kams knew them better than love, compassion or, for that matter, even hate. That constant longing for more, the hole that could never be filled and the enigmatic, ever-present fear that came with it. Some fools called these afflictions, but they were his friends and guides. The emptiness was his cheerleader, constantly urging him to gratify, pacify and appease. The fact is that it was the simple act of filling this gaping hole that ultimately made him the king of the world. He took the malaise that plagued the world and turned it into his ally, and he had not stopped patting himself on the back for it ever since. However – yes, there was a however – in an ideal world, he would have kept the greed and let the fear go, but sadly they are conjoined twins. And so while the avarice pushed him, fear made him pay the price – his bones ached, and the whirling in his gut never quite rested. However … yes, there is another; however, he did not let the fear destroy him. Instead, he propitiated it by destroying the world. Voila! Kams had danced this tango to perfection so far, but things were changing.

And today, fear had turned up alone, dragging along a much-debilitated greed. Without avarice, it was just pointless pain that radiated from his core to every muscle in his body. He wanted someone to knead it out. Instead, he was seated on his oversized throne, trying to devise a plan to stop what was supposedly inevitable. He looked at his loyal subjects, who were hanging on to every word he said. The severe pain travelled to his face and became a scowl. Uncharacteristically, Kams was no longer able to maintain the apparent machismo, and he signalled his attendants who needed but a hint. Four perfect-looking people covered his ample shoulders with their nimble pressing fingers. A few minutes of pounding and pressure later, his thoughts were somewhat released from the grip of inexplicable fear: 'We must waste no time. Now that we have a way in, let us prepare to go and attack that … and kill … what's-her-name.'

A compliant, dutiful courtier stepped forward to help his esteemed ruler. 'Her name is Krishna, oh dear king.' While it was evident to everyone else that it was not a question but an attempt to invisiblise his augured nemesis, this particular courtier had missed the cue. Luckily for him, there was no time for extended cruelty today. Kams had an army to lead. He knew he had to get on with finally destroying the single source of fear that followed him like his shadow. So Kams closed the matter with a look of utter contempt and some good old banishment, 'Get out and never be seen again.'

Morning in Ujwala was a time for thriving. The sun swept the valley, flowers bloomed, the river bustled with life, and people ambled their way to work. This unchanging routine had helped them get through an upheaval or two. This time too, they were hanging on to it for dear life, somewhat defeating its purpose. After all, pretend languidness is pretty hard and only serves to exaggerate the feeling of impending doom.

Krishna emerged from the tent with a flutter of foreboding in her heart. Like a sitting duck, she had to wait for Kams to make his move. She could only hazard a guess as to what Kams might unleash on Ujwala – or when. Honestly, the first mission could have been more straightforward.

Prince dug ditches around the portals. Ryan built barriers using concrete. Anita put her legion of plants to work to help obscure the possible entrances of the portal. And Maya had not slept a wink as she tried to find a mind from Kams's realm that she could plunge into to see what he was planning. They sat by the portal, exhausted but still alert.

Krishna had not tried to stop them even though she knew what no one else did. Time travel through the portal transferred energy that converted to matter only on its arrival. The laws of time travel were such that matter could not travel through the portal; only energy could! And the energy assembled into matter on arrival. Naturally, barriers made of ditches, plants and concrete could not stop energy. And yet the team continued to hover near the portals supposedly to guard the entrances. Krishna instinctively understood that her team was being propelled not just by the mission at hand but by the very thing that brought them there – they all wanted to time-travel. Desperately. Fervently. Krishna recognised that Anita's accidental hurtle ahead in time had further stoked this wish. Each of them had come to the team ostensibly for an altruistic reason, but their concealed motivations lurked and constantly threatened to waylay the mission at hand. Life is not perfect. Who knew this better than Krishna? She wanted to assure them that they would have a chance to heal what was past, but could not do it with any earnestness; she did not know where this evolving situation would lead them.

Maya felt her temples throbbing – as if her head were overheating. The pain spread like flames licking her brain, yet she could not give up. There in front was the portal – if it opened, perhaps she could jump in and go to the moment. *That* moment. She would stand in the way of death and block its access to Mo. She knew she would have that moment. She had to have it.

Anita refused to let the portal out of her sight. She had made it through once. Perhaps she was the only one, besides Krishna, who could time-travel. Anita had her secret mission and knew where and when she had to go; it was just the how. Thoughts ran ahead of her. A magnolia vine tugged at her gently to return to the matter at hand. She turned to stroke and soothe it, but kept waiting for the moment.

Maya's striving wasn't yielding anything but pain, and she noticed that it was not just her but Anita and Ryan too. They were all waiting. Waiting to change a moment, to make right what was wrong in their world. The larger world seemed so far away and undeserving. Some humans cast out and crushed others of their species on a whim – did they deserve saving? Shouldn't they save their own first? She reached out to Ryan and Anita, and heard what was in their minds – they would sacrifice any mission to turn back time. Her mind was overflowing, and Maya tried to order it, to filter and sort, but she wasn't fast enough and, without warning, a strange darkness enveloped Ujwala like an eclipse. The stench of chemical sewage permeated the air. Maya gagged as she turned to Krishna and saw her armoured up in her blue suit – waiting – and wondered what fresh hell was going to visit upon them. And with that, Team Krishna was called to the present.

Kilometres away from Ujwala, legions of men marched towards the field and Krishna Circus. They were armies deputed to destroy the circus and imprison its team – preferably in front of cameras. The advancing armies of 2024 followed the drill; the drivers barrelled forward in military trucks as the soldiers leaned out with their guns, so that everyone who saw them knew their purpose. It was not long before they were jolted out of their comfort. The drivers saw it first and were confused. They watched in horror as swishes of darkness hurtled past them and enveloped them in opaque fog. Panic replaced self-confidence, leaving them in a cloud of thick, polluted haze. Unable to see what was ahead, some speeded along, while the others stopped in their tracks. What was this unearthly adversary they were up against? *Is this the sun? What is this strange light?* The soldiers speculated as they gazed at the line of trucks framed against a murky neon-green light.

Kams spent a lot of time perfuming his body, but there was no way for him to wash what was inside, and it wasn't a real concern either. In his experience, people do judge books by their cover. So when he reached Ujwala, he was disgusted by the mud and dirt. Their 'lack of civilisation' made him pity these people. He had not yet found his form after he came through the portal. His energy was dispersed, dark and large as he loomed over the town and terrified everyone. Their quaint shops and quaking people bored him. His eyes scoured the little town to find the pesky woman he was there to kill. Ironically, the people of Ujwala scurried back and forth, trying to make sense of this strange darkness; sure that it was another one of Krishna's tricks, they blamed her.

Kams noticed a group that faced him – as if expecting him. Who were these handful of intrepid fools? One was a grown man, and the others were all children. His gaze shifted to the two children he recognised – they were the ones 'she' had risked her life to save. If the peacock-feathered pest was not here, the way to draw her was these midgets. He grabbed Eka and Jeet even as they struggled.

Now Eka was a small but strong girl who hated bullies; so she shouted at the dark cloud that had seized her: 'Put me down, you bully.' As Kams took form, Jeet threw a punch or two. Then Kams did something he never imagined he would do. He uttered her name. It was more like he bellowed loud enough for it to fill the ether: *'Krishna, I have come for you.'*

Krishna heard her name reverberating and took flight as her team made their way to the town square. Truth be told, Team Krishna put up a valiant fight, but the cards that Kams was holding were not in their pack. Krishna tried to free the children, but he had them in a grip that was tightening. She needed to make a decision, and so she went where she could make a good one.

Krishna envied the river that could flow on even as it carried the source of strife within it. She stood rooted as she faced the inevitable. Kams – the man who destroyed the world, murdered so many, who hunted down her parents, and the one whom she was augured to kill. Kams was her adversary and her life mission. What was she without him? Did she even exist without him? The wind blew a whisper gently into her ear and unlocked a memory.

Krishna and Yashoda had travelled to a time sixty-five million years ago when dinosaurs roamed the earth. Every moment was spent in the awareness that they were merely prey. Twelve-year-old Krishna was frightened and clung to her mother. 'Fear is but an impulse provided to us to help us save ourselves. It is advantageous when used correctly, because who wants to be eaten by wild animals?' Krishna could hear her own whispered answer: 'No one'. And she felt Yashoda as she encircled her in her strong arms: 'That's absolutely right! And so we, like all these animals, feel fear when there is danger. But do not invoke it when there isn't any present danger, or it will make you weak. Remember, the challenge must be met in the moment it presents itself, not in the past or future. So being present and attentive is all that is needed. It is simpler than you think.'

Krishna remembered sleeping deeper that night. Today it helped her accept what lay ahead. There would be another day to contemplate the predetermined nature of her life. Today was not that day. While her team tackled 2024, she would go to 2124 with Kams – as his prisoner. It was the only way to stop him – Krishna had to face her biggest fear.

Chapter 23

Return to Mathura

Youth is great. Never a wrinkle. No aches and pains. Money is the best. You can buy all you want. A full belly is so satisfying. Especially if the variety of food is tailored to your taste buds – literally. Who in the universe has an appliance that reads what you desire and provides it to you before you ask? That is what Kams had given them. But it did not feel like it was enough. Maybe it never ever is!

Mathura's residents were awaiting the spoils of war. They needed an offering to be reassured that the humdrum of falsehood would carry on forever. They waited with bated breath, and in anticipation of a win. They desperately needed confirmation that their choices were the right ones and that they had backed the right side.

Krishna knew that harm would come her way sooner rather than later, but when Kams went for the children, she lost all her bargaining power. There wasn't a moment to lose. She had to remove Kams before he changed his mind. She had earlier held Kams tight while freeing Eka and Jeet, and swept him and his army back to Mathura through the portal. Kams and his army made an unsightly heap, but Krishna was back in Mathura, armed with just her baton. The sight of her being airborne interrupted Kams's joy, but then she anchored herself to the ground and allowed his warriors to capture her. Mathura's inhabitants believed her surrender to mean that Kams had won. Some were disappointed, and others floated on in their ennui; but most cheered and whooped with joy. Kams brought them to attention as he announced: 'We welcome you to Mathura, the one who is just a girl.'

Krishna set her eyes on the man she was destined to destroy. There was no hyperbole in Yashoda's description. He was every bit the power-drunk ego-soaked man. His debauchery and decadence were not evident in his youthful, robust and shining body, but his eyes were pools of death.

Krishna felt something rising from the pit of her stomach, and it flooded her brain. Was this hate? She was immobilised; head throbbing and vision obscured by tears, she clenched her fists and held back the impulse to tear him to pieces. She hauled Yashoda's voice through her fogged mind and let it cut through: 'Never act in anger; it is debilitating and makes one ripe for losing. Anger will come … let it go. Conquer yourself before you conquer your enemy.' Krishna blinked and let the course of anger return where it came from. There, she dissolved it in her desire to serve and protect Mother Earth.

Krishna could not yet see the upcoming play of events, but she was sure of her first move – she needed to find Parshuram. As the blows came, she took them calmly while registering the perpetrators carefully – retribution without hatred was kosher even, according to Yashoda. They chained her heavily, giving her a good measure of how much they feared her.

Kams brimmed with mirth and arrogance. Even as the fear in his veins pushed him to kill her right there, he did not want to lose the chance for a spectacle that would finally put the last challenge to rest. Some of his most cruel soldiers surrounded Krishna, and he felt more invincible than ever. So Kams commanded: 'Parade her through the streets and throw her in the prison cell meant for her.'

As they carried her away, Krishna could still hear Kams issuing orders for a public hanging, preceded by torture. He listed in detail what they would inflict on Krishna. Even by his standards, it was cruel. His description gave the impression he wanted to recreate the crucifixion but with some added zing.

Krishna resisted nothing, even as she wondered about the bespoke cell and what it might entail. She had expected the punches, the sticks that struck her back and even the kicking that followed her fall to the floor. What she had not anticipated were the crowds straining with anger and hate. The rows upon rows of residents of Mathura – their faces free of age – abusing, spitting, grabbing and screaming hatred at her took her by surprise. Not a frown in sight, even as they encouraged the soldiers to rain pain on her; they jostled to participate in the spectacle and then, finally, the fury of the mob swelled, and her lynching ensued. Krishna had never felt this synchronised abhorrence, and nothing had prepared her for it. Her physical wounds would heal, but the hurt might be harder to repair. Strangely, Kams's soldiers saved her in the nick of time. Kams wasn't just going to let his subjects have all the fun.

They roughly pushed her till she stumbled into a hall that looked like a bank vault from 2090. There were endless identical, large, steel-grey doors in a slate-grey area. The spotlessness was shocking to the eye – such maniacal symmetry. There were no bars, and the only indication that there were prisoners behind the opaque cell doors, were the sounds of rattling chains, cries of pain and screams of torture. The guards knocked Krishna to the ground and dragged her. She took the time to take in the silver-grey floor and thought about the many hues of grey in the grim prison, and wondered how she was going to find Parshuram. Krishna spotted the sensors that lined the jail and made a note of their approximate direction. The guards unlocked one of the crypts, and she clocked the cameras that were trained on its entrance. Since subtlety was not the point of this exercise, they threw her in and slammed the door.

Inside the cell, she realised how it had been tailored for maximum discomfort. It was only big enough for Krishna to stand, and her ankles were chained to the ground. She looked up at the six-inch-square inlet for air and wondered how they imagined she could fly through it anyway. Her wounds were already repairing themselves, and she knew that would be an invitation for them to cause further pain.

Kams had personally laid out the order of torture, which was a mix of physical pain and mental humiliation. Krishna bore it well. Her body could self-heal, and she knew that. But her heart was not as immune – she felt a sense of fatality trickling through her bones. Eventually, the inventory was complete, and the guards left, exhausted and satisfied. They were wearing their actions like a badge of honour for a thing that only humans do – torture each other.

Krishna heard a new set of footsteps. Not surprisingly, they stopped outside her cell. The door of the chamber went from opaque to transparent, revealing Kams. He had come looking for the proverbial last conversation with his one and only potential destroyer. It was evident in the way an oversized throne-like chair was set just outside the door, and Kams seated himself in a 'for the long haul' sort of way. He raised one leg and ceremoniously placed it far apart from the other, thus opening his legs wide. He leaned forward as a predator would to its prey. Lastly, he dismissed his accompanying retinue to indicate that he alone was enough, notwithstanding the now transparent but indestructible door that stood between them.

Krishna sighed at this war dance that tangoed between sex and violence, where one could be freely exchanged for the other. Standing erect was making Krishna restless, and she wanted Kams to say what he needed to, and leave. But here he was, all settled and ready for the 'talk'.

Under Kams's deadpan face, Krishna saw the fear and hate bubbling. She watched as he spoke deliberately: 'I can see that you're very motivated by something a fool called Rudra predicted – that a "Krishna" born in Mathura would destroy me. So keen were they to have this fake prophecy come true that, when you were born in Mathura, they seized the opportunity, even though it turned out that you're just a girl. By naming you "Krishna", they have thrust upon you a mantle that is not yours. This is evident in the fact that you are here now … and imprisoned. And in a matter of hours, you will be dead.'

Krishna wondered if there was a kernel of truth in Kams's spew. What if she were executed right before all of Mathura? Would that be the end of it all? Was all this just a macabre cosmic joke? She tried to reach for Yashoda, but seemed inhibited by Kams's looming darkness.

Kams wondered if his words were taking effect as he continued to badger her in the way he knew best. 'Your little trick of taking flight is nothing we in Mathura can't get going. So, don't let these small baubles convince you of how special you are.'

Kams leaned back and watched Krishna as she sunk to the ground. The narrow cell forced her to fold on to the floor, as if she were an accordion, with the air pumped out of it. This was the position Kams wanted her in. From here, he could look her straight in the eye, but of course, he chose to look away, minimising her in the way he had practised for decades. Now he spoke in a gentle voice: 'See, every coin has two sides and every ruler, two facets. Today, I come to you with an offer from my generous and benevolent side. I offer you immortality and a life of comfort here in Mathura. Come and live with us as one of us or … you know … well …' He had measured every moment, and so this was when he would look up and meet Krishna's gaze for effect. He knew her face would be close to his, so he finished his sentence in a voice that echoed through the pristine prison: '*die*.'

Kams was doing well till the last overstatement. Now, Krishna looked at this swarthy man and wondered how very silly it would be to die at his hands. Plus, it seemed as if he had been stress-eating. The new folds on Kams's flesh made rippling patterns, slightly denting his predator image. Still, Krishna was in a cell, and Kams was not. Krishna knew that her lack of response peeved Kams. He wanted to hear her voice, listen to her pleading like the rest of humanity. And most of all, he wanted to know her. He wondered if she was the person he had imagined her to be.

And so he encouraged her, 'Now you may speak. This is your last chance to say what you would like.'

Krishna sighed as she weighed her words. She understood that, under the circumstances, her tone had to be placatory – something that would dial down the general wrath vibe. But then she spoke. It was in her voice, which seemingly had been hijacked by an unknown force: 'I will destroy you, Kams.' As the words left Krishna's mouth, she wondered why on earth she had said that, because she wasn't entirely sure if this was true. She wanted to soften the impact of her words and geared up for it, but instead, some other words tumbled forth without her meaning to, 'But don't worry, it won't happen any time soon. The formula is such: you will lose your power every time I reverse an event in history. The process will be long drawn. Prolonged.' Krishna was sure it was Yashoda channelling through her, thrusting her forward on her mission, and she smiled. Once again, it was a misplaced cue. She could see that was enough for Kams, and he rose with such force and anger that the chair was propelled down the narrow corridor as it tumbled and turned. His attendants came scurrying, and they quaked as Kams's ability to modulate his voice was temporarily suspended as he roared, '*I will be the one to kill you. You will die a painful death at my hands.*'

Krishna sat, still wedged, temporarily stunned as Kams slammed the invisible door with his fist, and it turned opaque once more. His shaking body took him back to a time when he was vulnerable. He wondered what had affected him so. After all, the girl was in prison … *his* prison. Then what was it? The answer threatened to disturb him further, so he pushed it away to an inaccessible corner of his mind, but it persisted: 'She speaks the truth, and you are no longer accustomed to hearing it. The truth is a scary place.' And then Kams stomped out, followed by his never-ending army of minions.

Chapter 24

Krishna's Prison Cell

Being alone and in charge is hard. Every decision has to be weighed in one's own mind. Is what I'm doing right? Can I even do this difficult thing that stands before me? No matter how much training and experience one has – it's always nice to have at least a bouncing board. On the flip side – the successes and failures were her own too. And that is empowering. Although is it? Hmmm.

Krishna – solitary in her metal box cell, with her body confined – found her mind generating thoughts against her will. New ones came and joined the pile without permission and destroyed years of mental discipline in an instant. She tried to order them, block them, but their obedience was not to be had. Her mind was flooded with thoughts of her team resisting an attack from an army equipped with weapons of mass destruction. Then there were the residents of Ujwala who had turned from believing in her to viscerally hating her. Krishna belonged to no world; but today, she was an outcast in all of them. But then there were also the children depending on her and her team to save their town – and future – from ruin. And Satya – he was there too. Satya, who made the colour rush to her face as if she had been running a lot. He made her feel as if she was the beacon at the centre of the universe, and also as if she had another half walking outside of her.

There was so much resting on what would happen next, and here she was, locked in a cell, more than a hundred years away. She looked for a clue to figure out how she might break out and found only a steel wall of nothing. She wished she had just a moment of clarity, stillness and quiet to make sense of what she was faced with, but there was no silence to be had. The horrifying moaning of the prisoners and the shrieks of agony continued unabated while she tried to think despite the grisly howls of pain. Like gusts of a storm, they were knocking her about even as she tried to sail through to reach just a single coherent thought. The well of guidance she had created with Yashoda seemed to have gone bone dry. She felt her years of training melting away as she sat crouched, paralysed by a maelstrom raging in her mind.

Krishna tried to unfold and straighten herself. She wanted to stand up and stretch, but was wedged between walls too narrow for her frame. Her bones ached with a craving to be set free. Her back felt as if it was carrying the weight of the entire world. Her arms felt like tremulous nothings. And her mind was swirling like a boat caught in an undertow. Her mind tried to push back; it reminded her that she was, after all, the augured saviour. There had to be some truth to that! The suggestion seemed to have a contrary effect, as a dam seemed to break its bounds and a gush came pouring in. Sounds from a television from a hundred years ago denouncing her as a terrorist; voices of people of Mathura hurling abuse at her, wishing death upon her, spitting at her; and the words of Kams and his soldiers became a booming cacophony that filled her head. Her chest heaved, and her breath quickened to combat this assault, but she was losing. Why did *she* need to be the one to save the world? She craved ordinariness as never before. She thought about all the people of Ujwala going about their daily lives, and she craved their mundaneness. Oh, to quibble and quarrel over banalities, to love and hate with cavalier worldliness and to have no mission in life. It just did not seem fair.

She was the one who was an orphan. She was alone in the world. Not a person to call her own – then why did *she* have to carry this burden? Even her 'mother' had abandoned her. What could be the worth of an individual with no one to call her own?

Krishna raised her eyes and looked up at the vent to see if she could catch a breath and saw strange darkness streaming through it; it came in like an odour – palpable but invisible. She knew then that she was enveloped in something terrible. She was in the thrall of doubt. Her faith was slowly being drained out of her, like blood from a slaughtered animal. It was dripping away and taking her life, one drop at a time. What was the guarantee that she was indeed the saviour? The only person who told her that was gone – Yashoda had left her in the lurch. All around her was a desert of scepticism that devoured faith and hope. Across centuries, they only had criticism to offer. And maybe they were right. How could so many of them be wrong?

Krishna felt a tear make its way down her face. She knew she should be conjuring up her baton and fighting this, but something within her wanted it all to end here and now. She was just exhausted. She sat still, waiting for everything within her to give up the fight, to just get up and leave the building, but even that was proving hard.

As Krishna willed herself to let go of her very essence and trade it for freedom, she had failed to take into consideration that her life was no meadow; it was a road winding up a hill with sharp corners and no guarantee of what lay on the other side. So, naturally, a moment later, a turn led to the proverbial twist in the tale of her life.

The noise of the tortured prisoners ceased, and a perfect humming sound filled her cell. Instead of feeling relief, she was overcome with panic. What was this fresh hell, she wondered. And what would follow this? Was this the calm before the storm that would drop her on a rocky mountainside of more pain? Trust, when shattered, gives birth to looming doubt, and Krishna was in its grip. Paralysed, she couldn't even distract herself enough to think of other things, leave alone fight the dread. But hope has its ways: even as her mind was racing on the tracks of defeatism and winning the competition of self-pity, a voice cut through it. It indicated neither what sex it was nor what nationality or religion, and all it said was, 'Breathe, breathe, b-r-e-a-t-h-e!' And as she tried to follow that diktat, it had the counter-effect. For a moment, Krishna thought she was choking as her breath seized completely. Then an ocean wave of air gushed into her lungs, and the force of the big breath made its way into every nook and cranny of her body and virtually hauled her up. She stood erect and looked on as the light from the inlet expanded to include her, and soon she was submerged in it. In its fold, she felt as if she was in a warm embrace, loved, whole and part of something so much larger than her own problems. All she could hear was silence. She had never heard such a perfect sound before. And from it came just one voice, asking the question Krishna was thirsting to hear: 'Krishna? Are you here?'

Krishna's eyes welled up. How did she know this was the voice of the man who had saved her life? How did she know this was the man who believed when no one else did? How did she know that he had the faith she so needed now? She spoke without waiting for any answers, 'Yes, Parshuram, I am.'

Krishna thought she heard a sob of relief before the sounds of agony resumed. The groaning and shrill cries of tortured prisoners – imprisoned by cells created only to deplete spirits – howled like ghosts haunting and hunting souls. The unbearable cacophony should have been the last straw, but Parshuram was here! And it was time for her to move. She touched the opaque door, closed her eyes and called with a fervour that made her heart vibrate like a drum struck with an unimaginable force; and there she was again, back to guide her and let her know that she would never be alone. Yashoda's voice was a whisper that stilled her heart. She said, 'Matter is real only to those who believe the dream of earthly reality; to you, it is just the creative force. A mere vibration – align with that which gives birth to these apparitions. Feel it. Know it. Believe what you know, my daughter, my precious child.' The caress of her mother's voice shifted something within her, and Krishna drew her breaths in the pattern that Yashoda had taught her. The familiar force made its way up her spine and sublimely exploded at the top of her head. A strong pull of light drew her from the point between her eyebrows. This always altered her vision, and she could see through matter. And when she opened her eyes, she saw clearly what she must do to be free.

It wasn't long before Krishna found what she was looking for. The small lever that controlled the door was so well concealed that only someone with her special vision could spot it. With some time, effort and help from her baton, she popped it like a bottle, and the door gently swung open. She stretched out her legs and walked towards the source of Parshuram's voice, 'Parshuram?' She did not need to wait long before a trembling voice answered: 'This way.'

Krishna identified the button that turned the cells from opaque to clear with the flip of a switch; the space was transformed into a roomful of dancing squares of light, and cross-currents of breeze streamed from the hundreds of light vents. Krishna had expected to see hordes of writhing bodies, but it was empty except for one prisoner – Parshuram. It turns out the sounds were designed to keep the ghosts of torture alive – a well-orchestrated mirage to obscure the truth.

Krishna had estimated the levels of torture Kams would have been inflicting on Parshuram but was still stunned by what she saw. His face full of healed and unhealed wounds, his hair overgrown and matted with bodily fluids, one shoulder had slipped lower than the other, and it was clear that one of his arms was broken as it hung to his side. He was trying to haul himself up from the hard plank that served as his bed, but his limbs did not seem able. Upon seeing Krishna, Parshuram discovered a reserve of energy that he did not know existed, and limped across the cell and touched Krishna's face with his calloused, bruised hands. It was the gentlest touch she had felt in a long time. Parshuram smiled, and it appeared that he might have healed just a little: 'Krishna – dear child.'

Rivulets of joy streamed down his creased face as he gazed upon the miracle that would save the world. Krishna wanted to hug him but feared hurting his brutalised body. So instead, she reached over, wiped the tears, and offered to carry him away. 'Come on, let's leave quickly.'

Surprisingly, Parshuram stepped away. 'No, Krishna. Now is not the time. I must stay here. There is more for me to do here.' Krishna could not imagine what might prompt Parshuram to stay in this pit of pain, but she had to trust him. He patted the hard surface while wiping it clean with the other hand and invited her, 'Come and sit with me.' In a grey room of swinging blocks of light, they sat a moment in silence, in appreciation of this much-awaited meeting. Parshuram gazed at Krishna as if searching her face for a secret. 'You were just a little baby when I saw you last. Look at you now!'

Krishna was expecting profound advice from a man renowned for his intellectual capabilities, but in the end, his words were that of an uncle. Krishna smiled – it had been a long time since anyone had treated her like a child. 'Well, it has been twenty-five years since you saw me last!' she smiled.

Krishna felt so much love as Parshuram laughed, exposing his semi-toothed mouth. She wanted to know everything he had been through, and they spent the next few minutes recapping their lives so far. Parshuram recounted the horrors perpetrated by Kams and how they were further exacerbated when Yashoda disappeared, taking Krishna with her. Kams's relentless search to find and destroy Krishna became an obsession, and Parshuram bore its brunt for obvious reasons. Then Parshuram wanted to understand where Yashoda took Krishna and what she learnt. Krishna summarised her life for him too.

Krishna wondered what had kept Parshuram going. She asked, 'Did you know that I would come here?' Parshuram nodded. 'I had an intuition. You see, Rudra revealed every detail of the augury only to me. And those were to be disclosed to you at the right time.'

'What is it that I don't already know?' Krishna asked. Parshuram sighed – he recognised that, augured messiah or not, Krishna was still a young woman with emotional scars, and he searched her face to ascertain how many of the truth cards he could lay bare. He spoke deliberately, 'Krishna, you cannot be killed. You are invincible; so, go into all battles knowing that … but you already know that?' Krishna nodded to acknowledge a fact her mother had often told her. She confidently pointed at her body, which had already healed every wound inflicted on her. And Parshuram knew he had to inform her: 'But … my dear child … guard your heels.' Parshuram saw fear flicker across Krishna's face as she instinctively looked down at her booted, encased feet. Parshuram reached out and patted her hand as he told her what she needed to know. 'Your death lies in your heels. If you know it, you can take care of it. Guard them, okay?'

Parshuram smiled as he saw Krishna rotating her ankles and wiggling her toes in her boots. She seemed to be feeling out this newly discovered vulnerability and nodded, trying to understand the import of those words. She was a superhero but with a weakness that could kill her. The fear returned momentarily, and she held Parshuram's hand. He decided not to interrupt the ingestion of a new revelation and patted Krishna's hand. She wanted to know: 'Why didn't my mother tell me this important detail when she told me everything else?'

Parshuram replied patiently, 'She did not know about this, Krishna. As I said, there are some truths known only to me.' The question that followed was to be expected: 'Does Kams know about this?' Parshuram wished he was not the one to deliver this news to her: 'Not yet, but he will find out in the future. In the meantime, you must learn to protect that part of your body and still be brave, as if you have no vulnerability.' Krishna nodded and felt reassured that she was safe, at least for now. Parshuram saw her lean back and look him in the eyes; she had so many questions and was going to ask them.

'What were my parents like?'

'I met them so very briefly, but they were brave and loved each other very much.'

Parshuram watched Krishna's face take a downward turn – she clearly wanted to know more. 'They were leaders like you, and fought very hard for you to be born. Krishna, you are a time traveller. Sooner rather than later, you will meet them yourself.'

His placatory promise put the smile back on Krishna's face, and he added, 'And you have the tent to help you go there, right?'

'About that – is there any way that the tent can tell us in advance where we are going and what our mission is?'

'The tent is yours. As you grow, so will the tent. It is programmed to evolve with you.' That made complete sense to Krishna, and she understood the tent a little better now. 'For example, after this little fiasco where Kams found his way to you, the tent will have learnt to close the portal when you return.'

On cue, in the distance, Krishna heard the sounds of alarms going off – her game was clearly up. It was time for her to go. This time, she did hug him. Parshuram winced with joy. Krishna had just enough time to make her way out of the jail before it once again became an opaque dungeon.

Out in Mathura, she decided to leave a message for Kams. She found the cold-blooded soldiers who had earlier felt free to hurt her. She bound them with rope and hung them metres above the ground on one of Kams's faux trees, with a note that read 'This is the beginning of the end'. Krishna's handwriting wasn't her strongest suit, and she hoped Kams would get the message. In any case, to seal the deal, she set Kams's palace on fire.

Kams watched the flames licking his palace walls as he read the note written by a woman who ought to be dead. He bellowed like a demon awakened from the depths of hell. He would frame the heads of those that let her get away. And after that, he would wait. He had all of eternity, and he was going to use it to devise ways to destroy Krishna.

Chapter 25

Of Mortal Men

Truth is the truth. Truth always triumphs. Truth cannot be hidden. Truth will set you free. But the lie gets halfway around the world before the truth has a chance to put its pants on. That is also the truth.

Satya felt as if his life was partial, incomplete. As if he were living with something taken from his body. Somewhere between leaving his life in the city behind and making Ujwala his home, he had given up on the idea of finding love. He had convinced himself that living free was better than being tied down by love. He discovered how little that freedom meant to him when he met Krishna. Empathetic. Other-worldly. Courageous. Saviour. Odd. Very odd. Alien? He was never sure how to define her, but he knew he loved her. Deeply. And now she was gone, with no date of return. The only certainty was that when and if she did arrive, she would ultimately depart, and this time forever. He was part of the first stop on her long journey to save Mother Earth.

While he struggled with this idea, he decided that, in the meantime, he too would play a part in fulfilling Krishna's mission. In fact, it was an endeavour every human being who's living off Earth's bounty ought to undertake. Satya knew he did not have an army. Still, he was not alone in his enterprise. He had a motley band of believers, starting with the little ones – Jeet, Eka, Rumi, Dhwani and Rahul – and ending with the sagacious, experienced Atmaram Gupta. With no superpowers at hand, they decided they would take the most human route of getting the truth out there – print, beam, stream it out!

It took one phone call and travelling time for Nikhil Mandal to reach Ujwala. This was his story, and no one was going to take it away from him. However, it was still an act of bravery. After he published what he saw in Ujwala, journalistic corridors buzzed with whispers about his 'crazy' story featuring superheroes. Some believed he had keeled over into a world of fantasy by ingesting intoxicants. Then there were others who cared only enough to laugh behind his back. Nikhil was an established, credible journalist, and the slander had cut deep. So, this time, he came armed with a video camera – he would show them!

Nikhil went after the story like a dog with a bone, refusing to let go until he got everything out of it. Satya knew that Eka and Jeet were exhausted with the effort of telling the story multiple times, and still, they soldiered on. He felt a deep sense of pride in their sense of commitment and bravery. Perhaps this generation would be the one to turn the tide, to choose generosity over greed, and the inhumanity could end once and for all. Still, it was hard to hold on to this idea with the noise of machines destroying Ujwala playing in the background. Ironically, this soundtrack of the collapse was just what Nikhil needed, and he urged them all to speak over the sound. Plus, he filmed every shred of evidence that he laid his eyes on. It was clear that he was going to cover every single aspect before he allowed his jaded colleagues to lay eyes on his story.

Nikhil spent many lonely hours editing and scrubbing through hours and hours of footage before he had what he considered thorough evidence of the events. As he played it one last time, he leaned back in his chair and sent out a prayer. Though he was an atheist in real terms, he decided to put his entire weight behind appealing to an unknown entity. He even closed his eyes as he imagined an all-encompassing being that could make every newspaper embrace his work. To make them stand up for what was right, to use the might of the media to repair what was broken.

Sadly, it did not work. As it turned out, news editors weren't willing to endorse a 'cock and bull' superheroine story that wasn't paid for by at least one political honcho. Nikhil had thrown his entire might behind the enterprise, and wasn't going to give up easily. So, he desperately clung to his mobile phone, either waiting or calling, and his hands ached from the effort. Not only did they not accept his story, but they also accused him of circulating fake news. They were sticking with running the 'anti-national' story for now. What was true for the sponsors was true for the television channels. Nikhil felt alone and, as the news day was at an end, he felt it transmuting into loneliness. At 9 p.m., he recognised that he was up against a large and unforgiving system.

Finally, he gave up and decided to upload the report – unadulterated and without catchy blurbs – on a few of his social media handles that had as many followers as did honesty. He stared unblinkingly and scrolled repeatedly in the hope that something would change, but nothing did. He distractedly thought about how he had been trying to bring his screen time down and that this constant checking and rechecking would mean that this effort was also shot to hell. Soon, he felt the pit in his stomach growing like the rising seas, threatening to engulf him.

He lay down on his single bed, gazing directly at his barely stocked kitchen. He needed a real job but, increasingly, jobs were hard to come by. Flooded with regret, he searched his mind for missed opportunities. He wondered how life would have been, had he taken that job in the IT Cell of a political party or if he had joined the Indian Administrative Services. The presence of curiosity and individuality in his personality had not served him well. Maybe his middle-class parents were right – there was no point in chasing one's dreams. As his father once said, 'Child, chasing dreams is like running after elusive girls; they show you possibilities, and then they disappear.' It was true that his father had a limited understanding of women and metaphors; even then, Nikhil's meandering remorse thought, *he could be right.*

Nikhil felt his breath shorten, his heartbeat accelerate, limbs tingle. A trench of nothingness formed in his stomach, and he whirled down into the vortex he regularly visited. It marked the point where he would lie prone for days, shedding tears for reasons that his mind had prearranged. He had no control over it – he could only weather the storm. He tried to conjure up his hero, B.R. Ambedkar, the man who fought against every odd – of caste, poverty and colonial rule – and came out on top. The man who ultimately authored the document that laid the basis of India as a country. The very constitution that was currently being flagrantly undermined and even erased.

The last thought propelled him out of his bed, and he sat up dizzy from dehydration. He drained a two-litre bottle of water and looked at his plastic alarm clock. It was 1 a.m. Time flies when you're having a panic attack. The pit in his stomach felt as if it held some heavy rocks. Lacerated by the grip of anxiety, he attempted to breathe deep and work up the nerve to inform Satya that his bid to help had failed.

Nikhil reached for his phone with unsteady hands and saw it in a state he had never seen. He scrolled through this phenomenon some would call 'blowing up'. What he didn't know then was that TV stations, websites and newspapers, who had earlier shooed him away, were tearing into the social media trends #saviour #superheroine #saveujwala #childrenformotherearth #Lobhathethief.

Nikhil's phone wasn't the only thing that was blowing up. Ujwala was quickly turning to debris even as the pressure from the media built up.

Ryan saw an advancing overreaction. He had expected a few military men, but instead, there was a battalion of soldiers, tanks and oversized guns. They marched forward with the dedicated purpose of destroying an enemy that had been fabricated. Unbeknownst to them, their target Krishna was roaming across various time dimensions while they marched on to a ratio of one to a hundred and their fear was still not quelled. Their amygdala was sparked anew when they spotted Team Krishna. Naturally, then they drew out the artillery.

Maya was amazed at how well Team Krishna worked together, despite being virtual strangers. Like a symphony, they played to their strengths – she divined; Ryan lifted and removed, but so gently that it might seem like he was handling glass; Prince dug deep to create ravines to separate them; and finally, Anita summoned flowering vines to contain them. Soldiers of the 2024 army had neither witnessed such powers, nor gentleness. Was no one trying to kill them? Maya would have laughed out loud, but her heart welled with sympathy for the confused thoughts that had thrown the men and their guns into such confusion.

Satya, Atmaram and the children watched the versions of reality that surged through the TV screens. It was a good sign that every politician worth his salt wanted to take credit for it. One of them skirted the truth when he said, 'Maybe Lord Krishna has returned to alleviate our misery.' Soon, the story was cast in different hues of political leaning. In 2024, the media was no longer a pillar but a bolster on which many leaned to elevate themselves; but they all agreed that the army sent in to capture Krishna had failed.

The boat of Lobha's sangfroid was shaken. He hated losing, and that's all that had happened since he set his eyes on Ujwala. The creases on his brow had become deep enough for ants to regard them as skateboarding venues. Many objects – such as paperweights, pencil holders and even cups – had been launched at his minions. There was also some catching at the collar, punches, slaps on the head, and verbal abuse.

Lobha knew only one way to play this out – escalate the matter and finish Team Krishna. So he picked up the phone to those he paid to be in power and asked them to go all the way. What the army could not do, the bomber jets would.

Chapter 26

Lemon Squeezy

Human beings! Self-proclaimed 'most intelligent species' on Earth. Does having a large brain, four limbs and the ability to walk on two of them define intelligence? I mean, why don't the octopuses rule the world? Maybe it's got something to do with how human beings define intelligence. Because it's clear that the most intelligent are not ruling the world – the most desperate to survive are. Otherwise, why would they need to travel through time, literally undoing the damage wreaked by the human species?

The tent felt the 'moods' coming on. Feelings that seemed to swing like a see-saw. Some would say it was in large part because it had not reached emotional maturity. Being fully aware of the unripe nature of its inner world of feelings, the tent wondered if what felt like extreme irritation could just be foreboding and trepidation. Krishna had been gone too long and too far, to a time and place ruled by a man who only wanted to see her grievously harmed. Why would she take that chance? And leave them bereft? There was no circus without her, and no adventures for the superheroes to go on. The tent felt itself deflating under the weight of all these worries. Then something that felt like a tremor went through it. A feeling akin to anticipation … hope! What was this coming through? Then a sigh of relief brought the tent back to its form when it became clear that it was Krishna making her way through the portal.

Her sojourn in Mathura made Ujwala feel like a cosy home. The tent flapped at her arrival, applauding her return and welcoming her into its fold. Although eager to see the state of affairs in 2024,

Krishna still took a moment to feel the surface of the shelter – its cool surface, which felt just like a tarp before, now felt like a breathing organism, and Krishna felt a deep connection with the tent for the very first time. She wanted to lie in its folds, but realised the tent was empty. She did not know the whereabouts of her compatriots, and she was going to wing it and find out.

Hovering over the field's periphery, she found stragglers of a beaten army that was sent to destroy Krishna and her team. Ironically, those who had come to save the world from destruction had been labelled anti-nationals, and orders issued to annihilate them. However, those tables had turned and Team Krishna had done their job well. But why was there no jubilation?

Anita was the first to spot Krishna as she swooped down to join them. Krishna listened intently, and she realised the fight was not over. Lobha was not giving up and had connived with the political powers to order a bombing from the air. They wanted Team Krishna dead, but weren't really concerned about the devastation it would cause to Ujwala and its people. To Lobha, it was collateral damage. Krishna thought about how avarice and lust for power united men across time. A part of her wanted to introduce Lobha to Kams – they had so much in common! But this was not the time and space for it.

Krishna knew that she and her team could handle the situation at hand, but she feared for the mortals on their side – Satya and the children. Where were they? Maya saw Krishna's fear and immediately knew the question on her mind. She said in response, 'They're on TV – making a ruckus, rabble-rousing and bending public opinion.' 'Well, of course, they are!' Krishna shook her head, both in admiration and relief.

What Krishna did not know, but Lobha did, was that Atmaram had joined Satya and his band of minor warriors to rabble-rouse and flood every screen with 'The Truth'. They also had that journalist called Nikhil something-or-the-other on their side – a scribe who ought to have been written off years ago; an outdated dinosaur who still schlepped his way to stories when he could just sit in one place and wait for a press release like everyone else. Lobha felt the futility of all this 'civic' action. He was sure that Nikhil's media ambush would not stop the government from ordering bomber jets to control acts of violence of an anti-national like Krishna. There were laws in place for such things. And it wasn't uncommon for the ruling classes to ignore public opinion as if it were a pesky mosquito to be swatted. He scoffed gleefully as he read the email marked 'important'. There were orders to arrest Krishna and her team to 'better understand their abilities and the concept of time travel'. Then, with some dismay, he realised that they wanted Krishna and her team alive. This was confusing for Lobha. How could you bomb them while simultaneously keeping them alive?

He punched his phone harder than needed and succeeded in not dialling the correct number. He decided bellowing was easier, even if one had to do it repeatedly like a foghorn to bring all to heel. In less than a minute, someone shuffled in, only to inform him that there were instructions to cease military action immediately. Lobha received the news with his signature petulance, but this time he decided to go a step further – he would do what needed to be done, on his own. The charade had gone on for too long, and he was going to be the one to put an end to it. His temper tantrum had necessitated that Mukesh Mehta be summoned. Someone had to bear the brunt of his unfulfilled dream. MM, in turn, dragged Vijendra Gupta along – he was damned if he was going to bear the brunt of Lobha's anger on his own. Vijendra felt forced to participate in what was clearly a suicide mission.

Lobha decided to start with a tongue-lashing, stopping right on the border of grievous physical harm. Then he instructed Mukesh Mehta to personally ready a bomber plane quickly, while the orders to stop the jets were still roaming the long-winded corridors of bureaucracy. Enough time for him to move in, take control and do what needed to be done. He was not to be defeated. That was the only rule of thumb, and MM held on to it for dear life. Consequently, Lobha walked, scurried and then finally ran while Mukesh Mehta and Vijendra Gupta tried to keep pace.

Vijendra Gupta had not quite signed up for taking over bomber jets; so he dithered and did what was natural to him and lied: 'Sir, I have a fear of flying.' Lobha watched as he made all the movements of boarding another aircraft but instead made off to the side, huddling and scampering. Lobha's arched brow marked him for another day, but Vijendra Gupta did not stay long enough to look back and see it.

Somewhere in Lobha's deluded mental ecosystem, he was not just getting into an aircraft, but undertaking an act of heroism; and Mukesh Mehta's loyalty was a confirmation of just this. *Heroes attract a blind following*, he thought. In Lobha's mind he was not pushing the pilot off with force but removing an impediment to his hallowed goal. And that was not the horrified expression of a pilot hitting the tarmac but the face of the enemy. Lobha was always so convinced that it soothed Mukesh's heart, and the latter sidled closer to his boss while Googling 'how to fly a bomber jet' – this activity of reading off the internet and flying a plane was clearly not working. Lobha watched MM beg and coerce the pilot back into the cockpit, and thought how much this was like making alliances – a thing that all leaders do.

The pilot took control and they made their way to Ujwala, he leaned back in his seat while MM noisily enquired where the parachutes were, and how many. Flying above the earth and amongst clouds did something strange to Lobha – he felt his mind lifting with the aircraft. There – away from his self-created Mecca of materialism, distanced from the ground where so much was always at stake, and where his only reason to be was to amass power – he felt overcome with something that felt like a warm whispering breeze. It disturbed him greatly, because he had never felt this distancing and detachment from the goal he had been avidly seeking. He needed something to shake him out of this strange state. He looked out of the window at the clear sky, littered with flouncy clouds. Against this ethereal backdrop, the woman in a blue suit with her peacock feather headgear seemed to float and glide. Lobha was squarely and rudely pushed back to his seat of fear, greed and anger. He tried to encourage the pilot to let loose the killing explosives, but could not convince him to do so at the wrong targets. After all, they were still some distance away from Ujwala. And so he helplessly watched as Krishna used her super strength to force the planes to descend towards the earth and heard her as she screamed over the sound of the distressed aircraft machines: 'Use the parachutes.' Lobha could have reached out and strangled her, but for the strong winds and the pilot encouraging him to jump before it was too late.

As Lobha and Mukesh Mehta floated down – the wind in their hair and their clothes flapping like a bird's wings – Mukesh Mehta smiled, for he was alive and sailing down alongside Lobha himself. He was closer to him than ever before. A near-death experience can do that. At that moment, MM thought he knew what it felt like being in love. On the other hand, Lobha was more focused on keeping his gaze straight, and tried not to wiggle his legs. It was his only chance at saving his suspended dignity, and he would be damned if he let himself down again. He held his body still, but his mind was ticking faster than a time bomb, churning to give birth to another scheme – something equally devastating and moneymaking.

Chapter 27

No Long Goodbyes

Change is the only constant but it always surprises us. We want things to stay the same but are quickly bored when there is no change. How is it possible to feel that each day has something new to offer and yet absolutely nothing changes? The answer is – Love. When there is love, every moment feels novel.

Satya had watched the sun set over Ujwala for precisely 1,448 days. In a few days, it would be four years since he first saw the sun make its way beyond the horizon and scatter its receding rays on the town. Most of these were peaceful and predictable evenings, and marked the time for withdrawal and regeneration. He had looked forward to these moments and had wished for them never to change, but at the time, he was not aware of what was bubbling under the field. Something had been averted. As a result, his life had been transformed. He was no longer craving peace; because, through all the turmoil, he had found it. His mission had expanded from his selfish need for something more significant, and he no longer wanted to lose this new-found sense of purpose. He had the feeling that he wasn't the only one who felt this way – the unexpected outcome of the events had left Ujwala's residents quiet but grateful. A light breeze swept through Satya's bee garden and brought the news that Ujwala had transcended its ordinariness – it had survived to tell a story that would inspire many others. As a result, not one, but several man-made disasters had been averted, inspiring others to rise and fight for what was right.

Behind him, he heard those who now had a greater chance of inheriting a greener planet. Jeet's request to set up the telescope reminded Satya that a handover was in order. He turned to face the voice and found that Jeet was accompanied by Eka, Rahul, Rumi, Dhwani and Krishna, who seemed to fit right into the group of children.

Satya brought out the telescope, now neatly packed in wooden boxes, and presented it to them with a flourish, as if at a prize-giving ceremony: 'This is for all of you; because you are courageous.'

Eka's nagging intuition warned her that an ending was on hand, and she reached over and embraced Satya. Satya blinked back tears as he heard her whisper 'I love the bees'. It wasn't long before the others joined in, and for a moment, they stood in a group huddle under a sky that was quickly revealing all its stars. Satya and Krishna could sense that the little ones weren't willing to let this moment end. The only way forward was to spin a yarn, tell a story that would bide time and help them forget what was imminent, until their bedtime. Soon after, nodding heads indicated that sleep was claiming them. Krishna and Satya brought the half-asleep children to their homes, where their parents received them with gratitude.

That night, on a long table lit with lanterns, Satya saw a group previously torn apart by strife, but who were now breaking bread. Looking at Krishna, he felt a renewed love for the catalyst that had made this possible. The celebration feast, hosted by Amir and Rabia Hussain, brought together Team Krishna, Atmaram Gupta, the Rathores and the Mehras. Food and conversation flowed freely, but no one was willing to address what the new day would bring. Everyone suspended the belief that this wouldn't last forever. So, conversations stayed strictly in the present and about current events and the people involved. The surprise came in the form of Vijendra Gupta and his wife. His remorse and apology were accepted even before it was voiced fully.

The tinkling of glasses and cutlery formed the background score for an evening that coursed with joy, remorse, forgiveness and a feeling of impending separation. Toast upon toast was raised till everyone reconciled to the inevitable. The sun was planning its eminent return when all parties made their way to their respective beds.

Eka woke up the next morning and drew back the curtains. She always wondered why they painted the sun like a yellow football in the sky. To her, it was a smudge that coloured the entire scenery with deep yellow, white, blue and sometimes an orange hue. She felt perplexed by the reaction she received every time she drew it as such – was it that adults wanted reality to fit into the shapes they knew? Round, triangle, rectangle or even a straight line. How she hated that she needed to colour within prescribed lines – it seemed like a complete lie. These thoughts played in her mind as she prepared for a day when she knew the sun would be scattering itself on every little piece of Ujwala. She slipped on her shoes and ran out to see everything restored and pristine in her town. She didn't know what this meant. Was Krishna still here? Did Satya stay? Eka's hair was unbound; as was her curiosity. She ran towards the field to find that Jeet, Rahul, Dhwani and Rumi had made it before her. The grass whistled as if calling out to them. The trees waved and bent in joy at their arrival. Under a clear blue sky, they saw that the field was just as it was before the circus arrived – empty and clear. Eka searched for some trace of Krishna Circus having been there – a reminder, perhaps? Something to remember what happened. Maybe she could write about it? Or would making drawings about Krishna Circus be better? She wanted to confirm with Satya which was the right way to go, and her feet carried her on this thought to Satya's home, only to find that his bees were finding homes away from their boxes. They buzzed, trying to tell Eka about the night before, about all they had seen. Sadly, she could not understand as they talked over each other. Eka found a box of bees – intact and with her name on it. 'Eka, this is for you'. It was signed *Satya* in broad, expansive handwriting. Where was he? Why did he leave?

Jeet kicked stones. It was his coping mechanism to get rid of the feeling of 'missing'. Rumi, Dhwani and Rahul watched him do this as they ambled over to the school. Jeet had a moment to wonder where Eka had run off to when he spotted her walking towards them with a box raised above her head; the shiny, cackling river framed her as if she had risen from the water. *It isn't just a box*, thought Jeet. *It is a mantle she carries, a purpose handed to her*. And he knew she would do this with aplomb. Jeet knew that all Eka did, she did with certainty, or not at all.

They held the box of bees by turns and resigned to the fact that Satya, Krishna, the circus and the entire team were gone. The moment was broken by the familiar voice of Ravi Sharma – their infrequent teacher and a man who was easily peeved by the long faces that greeted him. 'Hurry up. You have a lot to learn. Otherwise, you will always remain the helpless children that you are,' he bellowed, thus confirming that he did indeed live under a rock. Still, Jeet was thankful for their teacher's ignorance because it brought back the laughter, which further annoyed Ravi: 'Yes, yes. Laugh, laugh. Stupid children … don't know anything. What do you know? You are helpless and understand nothing. You probably think there is nothing out there.' He said this while pointing above, although he meant it to indicate the larger world. This pushed the children further towards convulsive laughter.

Krishna was aloft again in a tent that seemed steadier as it made its way through time and space. She wondered how and whether those in 2024 would remember her. She knew that her life would never be the same again. For one, there was a man stretched out by her side, smiling in his sleep as his hands were intertwined with hers. She had struggled with love on the one hand and her life as a saviour on the other. In the end, she had left the decision to the tent and was relieved when it acquiesced.

Satya awoke briefly, as if to convince himself that this wasn't a dream, and fell back into a secure slumber.

What more does a mother want than to see a happy and successful child? She wants to see her safe and protected. At another point on the time continuum, in another part of the universe, Yashoda stood in her signature straight-backed stance, watching her little girl's tent as it made its way across time to another mission. Yashoda might have been a fugitive on the run, but she was still a mother. And nothing gave her more joy than to see her child fly and find her wings, even as she kept a close eye on her.

Krishna could never understand how Yashoda made her way into her thoughts when she needed her, but she wasn't complaining. She cherished these visits and hoped that soon … *someday*, she could meet her in the flesh and have her at her side. It would be wonderful to have her mother – who always knew what she should do next to guide her on her missions.

After days and nights of idyllic floating, Krishna and Satya awoke to a flutter that she had now come to recognise; but this time the tent seemed to tremble with anticipation. Within moments, Anita, Maya, Ryan, Prince, Satya and Krishna assembled to watch the circus descend once more. This time, they were ready, willing and sure.

'Ah, here we go again. Does anyone have an idea what year it is?'

The tent fluttered. It had to find a way to tell them what it knew, but that could wait until they landed.

Epilogue

Palace of Mirrors

Defeat. How and where did this term enter the lexicon of Mathura? God knows what I would need to do to be just simply invincible. What's a man supposed to do when even immortality is not a given. Nature and her forces are to blame.
Damn them.

Kams sat silhouetted against an oversized window that streamed a hazy light into his sprawling quarters. If one ignored the fact that the haze was on account of Mathura being remorselessly set on fire, it might appear that the light was tailored to hide imperfections – especially lines, frowns, wrinkles ... the ravages of age, the signs of the onset of mortality. Kams's breaths were short; as if trying to keep up with the augured-but-all-the-same new situation. The monarch who believed in his immortality, who had time and again had this belief confirmed by events on earth, was confronted with the brutal truth of Rudra's augury, even though he was now just an apparition! Mohini's heart stirred with sympathy for Kams's shaken self-confidence. Still, she also understood the inevitability of actions having reactions and reactions having further reactions. Like mirrors facing each other, this endless boomerang was the basis of all reality. She pulled herself back from the rabbit hole of philosophy. She shuffled the nine yards of fabric that draped her and tinkled the glass bangles on her wrist. It was an attempt to attract his attention to the alcove, where she stood tentatively leaning into the emperor's chamber.

Kams was absorbed in thought and heard nothing. He was making a Herculean effort to plunge deeper and deeper into his mind to find stability, but he saw only confusing, swirling darkness. He wondered why he could not access his deepest, most profound and perhaps inspiring thoughts. Where were they? Had Krishna taken those too? Was it some trickery? Or maybe there really weren't any? Was he still even capable of it? Kams felt vulnerable. His short breaths did not help as he desperately tried to restore his hubris. He glanced over at his bed, which was in a state he had never seen before – empty! Running his hand over the sheets – perfect, soft, scented – he sent up a silent prayer of thanks that he did not need to pretend. He wanted to be unashamedly disappointed, angry, sulky, weak and irritated. He wanted to lie on the empty expanse of perfection and never get up, but his bladder nudged him to do otherwise. With no idea how to handle the bodily changes, he got up too quickly. The creaking sounds were imperceptible, but the pain was not. He looked down at his noisy knees, and at the first palpable sign that Krishna had indeed succeeded. He lay down again – defeated. Staring at the ceiling, he wondered what the people of Mathura were talking about today.

Kams could have wallowed all day in his reverie of self-destructive thoughts, but he was interrupted by someone calling out to him in a whisper. Alerted by the sound, he craned his neck and saw a courtier standing semi-concealed in a niche in his sprawling room. As his eyes adjusted, he noticed a person with a restrained manner, standing tall and draped in a saree that sparkled with so many colours that it seemed as if she were wearing a rainbow. Her symmetrical face and almost perfect body leaned tentatively, asking for his approval to speak. Strangely, he could not place this extraordinarily beautiful transgender courtier. He wondered how he had missed her, and whether he had lost sight of other things in Mathura. Summoning enough strength, he asked, 'Who are you and what do you want?'

Mohini had not accounted for the nervousness she felt at finally being in the presence of the high and mighty Kams. She answered, 'I … I am Mohini, your humble subject. Your highness … Mathura awaits you. It has been a week since people saw you, and they are beginning to worry…'

Kams wanted to turn his back and fall into a long slumber. He simply did not want to face a room full of courtiers whose individuality he had personally crushed. He had no wish to parade himself in front of those non-people. It was too cruel to have defeat detailed on his body for the entire world to see. Mohini saw Kams slump further into the morass of his large, empty, and perhaps a too-soft bed. She ventured to tempt him with the entourage she had brought: 'Your Highness, the ladies await you … to dress you themselves.' Kams felt strangely insulted by this childish offer to distract him; so he only deigned to raise his hand to dismiss those waiting. He waited to hear the retinue recede before shuffling to his never-ending closet that housed his clothes, ornaments and mirrors – which had previously always confirmed his invincibility. Today, he wanted to come face-to-face with what lay ahead. He summoned all the vestiges of bravery within him, and commanded the lights to fade in gently as they illuminated his biggest fear. He looked into the mirror expecting to see a monster afflicted by mortality, but what he saw left him confused. He looked even more youthful than before, perhaps as in his twenties. Only his eyes told of his experience; nothing else betrayed his actual age. It was an incredible turn of events!

Perplexed, Kams wondered how and whether this was possible. He felt the blood pumping in his veins and claiming youth once again – like it had been doing for years. He stared at his image, and the raffle of thoughts in his mind turned and threw up a new set of questions: How could this be? Could it be that his fear had clouded his brain? Had he only imagined the decay of his immortal body? What other way was there to tell than a reflection? What was more valid than what one could see and visually perceive? Nothing! Nada! Nothing at all! His breath deepened as he acknowledged the fact staring him in the face – he had defeated *the* augury!

Mohini looked on with some satisfaction as the monarch of Mathura squared his shoulders and claimed his position as the king of Mother Earth once again. He had a purpose in his gait and, soon, he would be back in court with the people who needed him to tell them who they were, what they stood for, and where. Sometimes solutions are simpler than you think.

Kams spent some time judiciously choosing his attire. He commanded the water to run full speed and fill a bathtub designed to accommodate more than a dozen people. Bottles and bottles of scents that could wash away any sin lined the walls. He hurriedly grabbed the vetiver and emptied copious amounts into the water. He submerged himself into the comfort of perfect temperature while mulling over a speech for his return. He would rouse them, assure them, and make his loyal subjects believe in him. He would stand as living proof of his success. His youthful body would tell of his victory. A strange feeling flooded his veins – was it gratitude? Or was it the bath salts making him feel fuzzy and the water hazy? Whatever it was, it made him bow his head in recognition of that which was protecting him. A sense of relief washed over him. He was supported by forces much bigger than him. Or was it just he and his unending power? Was he the ruler of the universe that determines the survival of all nature's creatures? In the end, he surmised that it was true. It was all he – Kams – the undefeated monarch of Earth.

Lost in his reverie, Kams gazed upon the slowly swirling bath water and saw the bubbling reflection of a much older man. Who was this person, he wondered. On closer inspection, it dawned upon him that it was he … only an older version, with salt and pepper specks in his hair, skin brittle and marked with age. The warmth seemed to drain from his body, and he felt a chill coming on, like a predator crawling under his skin, eating away at his body. Startled, he stumbled out of the bathtub. He commanded the tub to empty itself immediately. As the deceitful water disappeared meekly, Kams oversaw its draining. He was still immortal, and no water in a bathtub could tell him otherwise. He determined to permanently remove the bath salts and all those who conspired to stock them here. They were undoubtedly the same people who poisoned him to instigate the pain in his joints. He would find someone he could trust, and wall away all those who could be plotting to age him. He needed someone who wholeheartedly believed in his immortality and who knew how to keep his confidence bolstered. His mind went to the trans woman who seemed to still be in his room – she was present just enough for Kams to know she was there, but not so much as to intrude.

Mohini announced the king's impending arrival to his court, which waited for him like a flock awaiting their shepherd. They sat with ramrod straight backs, staring into the infinite distance, refusing to turn to each other and confirm their dented immortality. Mohini knew that, in Mathura, there was no necessity to speak the truth. If everything was built on an illusion, what purpose would it serve to point out its fabricated nature? Dishonesty must be maintained at all costs. And from here on, they would be bound to each other even more firmly, not just as citizens but as co-conspirators. Their pact would be sealed with a handshake, never to voice what was plain to see. With their gradually balding heads, greying tresses and skins that were beginning to comply with gravity, the citizens of Mathura were determined to fake it and hopefully make it. It was much better than accepting that Krishna The Brave came and set their city on fire. *Shush*, said Mohini to her mind; this was not the time to go there!

Mohini led Kams into court. He was dressed like a grand emperor – the crown was larger, the gems heavier, and the garments that draped and concealed his body were woven from actual gold thread that was most precious in a time when all riches had been sucked from the earth. Perhaps this was more ostentatious than was required in a court that was happy to receive whatever was dished out to them. They had been trained to not so much as flinch at his grey sideburns, the fine lines and the not-so-supple skin. In accordance with Mohini's instructions, they bowed and scraped as if it was business as usual, never directly looking at him. Kams, in turn, did them the favour of ignoring what he saw. In doing so, the deal was sealed, and a new age of camaraderie was heralded in Mathura; now, the subjects and their ruler could tell the same lie that Krishna had not dented their immortality, that they had not aged as a consequence of Krishna's actions in another century. Their existence was based on the premise of living forever and nothing was going to change that.

Satisfied, happy and restored, Kams looked around at the palace that had been rebuilt after being torched by the person whose name would never be spoken again. He was especially appreciative of the new court decor, and complimented Mohini for the many mirrors that had replaced its walls and ceiling. Beautiful, large pieces of reflective glass lined every surface of the palace. No matter where one turned, one could see one's true self staring back. All they saw were ever-youthful and immortal reflections.

Mohini soaked in the praise she received for this gift of youthfulness that she had enabled. Now, only youth reflected back at Mathura. Age? Hell no! I mean, what is that? Mohini's life's work of creating mirrors that would only reflect youthfulness had found its time and place. She humbly offered it up to Kams, who gladly accepted this new invention which highlighted his kingdom's commitment to youth and immortality.

Kams felt his chest swell with pride, but he couldn't catch a single person's eye. He sensed that they did not entirely share his enthusiasm and optimism. The air was heavy with their fears and simmering anger. Like cheated customers, they were no longer willing to buy what was being sold to them this time. Still, the fear was alive, which would keep them in line – at least for now. *This is all her fault.* Kams's utter abhorrence for Krishna was rekindled. He was determined to find and dismember 'her' at the earliest opportunity. If that creature thought she was invincible, she was not quite acquainted with his entire range of abilities and willpower. He would find her Achilles heel, and when he did, no superhero suits or powers could save her. She would be dead. Exterminated. Annihilated. This was the goal he lived for now. His *ikigai*, which he had lost for oh-so-long. For now, Kams had only one choice – to launch into the best speech he could come up with. The courtiers did their part and listened. They kept up the learnt applause and vigorous head nodding with seeming attention and belief.

Job done, first step taken, Mohini did what she had been doing all her years in Mathura – she tuned out. Her mind drifted to where it always did – to the state of the planet. She was a ruthless survivor like all the others in Mathura, but she had never stopped wondering why humans kept going when no other creature could survive. And whether Krishna could indeed bring back what was lost. And if *she* was the only one in all of Mathura who noticed that there was a strange sight – of rolling *real* green leaves at the edge of the see-through dome. They seemed to have been tugged away from revived saplings by the howling gales that haunted Earth's dusty surface. She longed to see and confirm the existence of these sources of hope that had come knocking at Mathura's periphery. Fluttering and colliding ever so lightly against Mathura's transparent shield, they came announcing the first signs of their revival – and the resumption of the cycle of birth and death. Was this restoration trumpeting Krishna's first victory? Mohini searched the faces of those assembled and wondered which of them still possessed enough courage to face what was already knocking on their doors, and found not one person. She dreaded becoming them – the faceless, spineless mass that merely survived.

Mohini stepped away and found a quiet corner. From inside her bustier, she drew out a delicately engraved mirror that would never stop reminding her of what was true. She gazed into it and spotted what she was looking for – her deepening crow's feet and fast-forming laugh lines. In her reflection was proof of the fact that Mother Nature was still here and her instruments – death and birth – were still at work. Mohini sighed with relief.